Dear Mr DJ

Maggie Fogarty

THANKS:

A big thank you to my test readers, Jane Kennedy, Spencer Smart and Sheila Willis. Your honest feedback was much appreciated.

And an extra big thanks to Spencer for the cover design.

I'd also like to thank my husband Paul for all his support and help with the book formatting.

Finally, I'd like to thank our cockapoo dog Bonnie for her great company as I slave away in front of the computer screen and for encouraging me to take regular walkies!

Maggie Fogarty

Chapter 1

Take one dramatic phone call followed by a radio talk show. Then throw in a request for an old cheese scone recipe.

These are the catalysts, the prompts if you like. The beats leading to a new beginning, a leap into the unknown.

I'm still thinking about the phone call when I park up at the side of the road to listen to the radio, to concentrate better. The interviewer is disconcertingly chatty and at odds with the serious subject matter.

'So what age were you when it happened?'

A pause, a quick intake of breath.

'Er – 14, just turned 14. I was on a school day trip to my local rep theatre.'

Another pause, this time too long for a live radio show.

'Take your time. I know this is a difficult subject.'

I hate his phony sympathy, the lowered voice. We all know what Mr Radio Host *really* wants to say. Get on with it. We need to hear your story in nice neat chunks to run seamlessly into the One O'clock news break.

A man taking pride in his smooth programme transitions.

'Sorry, I'm just a bit nervous. Er, I stayed behind afterwards to ask a few questions. At the time I was, you know, interested in becoming an actress. He seemed really nice and signed the back of my autograph book. Then he poured me a drink.'

I notice how she sounds high pitched and girl like. A teenager in a middle-aged woman's body.

'A drink – you mean an alcoholic one?' Mr Radio Host raises his voice to become suitably outraged.

'Yes, champagne he said. It tasted nice, a bit like fizzy pop. I suppose I must have drunk it too quickly because I started to feel giggly, a bit light headed like. He thought it was funny and poured me another. Er, that was when it happened.'

'And what did happen?'

Here we go. The killer nugget before we're catapulted into the break. The cliff hanger to keep us all listening.

'Well he lunged at me and forced his tongue down my throat. I thought I was choking, I couldn't breathe. It was horrible.'

'Horrible'. A strange little word.

Her voice is becoming more agitated, a memory being relived and presented to the listening nation in lurid technicolour. Suddenly I feel grubby, ashamed that I'm so engrossed in this anonymous woman's story. A story spanning over thirty years.

The host lowers his voice.

'You must have been terrified. Now if you stay on the line we'll get back to you after the news headlines.'

I switch off the radio. Enough. With the turn of the car key, my phone vibrates with an incoming text. I smile as I see it's from Amy. A message from my lovely daughter can never be ignored.

'Mum could you text me that recipe for cheese scones? My uni mates have chowed all the ones you gave me and have been raving about them. I thought I'd try cooking some myself.(Lol) Ta mum – love you loads xx.'

Amy, who has never cooked a thing in her life, now asking for a favourite family recipe? A sign that she is finally growing up? Of course I already have it off by heart but also know exactly where the original is written down. And it's high time that my daughter is given a copy of her own culinary history, passed on through the generations. A handing over of the baton.

This is all well and good but there's a problem. At the grand old age of fifty-three, I need to overcome my fear of heights to get to that little red recipe book.

As stupid as it sounds, I've never ventured up into the loft of my rambling 1930s Truro house and neither have I wanted to. But 'here's the thing', as Amy would say. The 'For Sale' sign went up yesterday and already there are five viewings lined up. Yes, five. My stomach lurches at the thought of strangers tramping through my house, weighing up the pros and cons, assessing whether their lives can now blend seamlessly with mine.

That's what happens doesn't it? One set of lives vacates a place to be replaced by new faces, voices, décor. It's a merger of sorts whether we like it or not. Common ground by way of bricks and mortar.

The loft had always been David's place, somewhere to escape from the female mafia of mother and daughter. Every so often, he'd disappear up the pull down ladder and emerge triumphantly with an old vinyl record, Christmas decorations and dusty photo albums. Occasionally he'd have what he called a 'proper clear out' but only ever rearranged things. There was never any evidence of things being thrown away. I'd laugh it off with 'liar, liar pants on fire' and he'd grin in that sheepish way of his. How I'd love to see that grin again.

Just once.

It's been three years since David left our home giving me the usual wink and peck on the cheek. I recall him shouting 'good luck' to Amy who was doing some last minute revision for her exams and her jokey reply for him to 'sod off'. Afterwards I spent hours trying to go over that morning. Was there a clue that something was amiss? Did he look paler than usual, more stressed? The answer always came back the same.

No. Absolutely no.

The day started like so many others in our twenty-five years together. Routine but comfortingly so. Truth is nothing was out of the ordinary in what would turn out to be an extraordinary day.

June 7. It was a Tuesday. As the rangy young police officer stood in the kitchen I could see the date ringed on the fridge calendar. My handwritten note danced before my eyes. 'Amy English exam. Collect dry cleaning. Book table at Carlo's for 7.30pm.'

The minutiae of everyday life turned upside by what the medics call a 'massive cerebral stroke.' The young officer was doing his best to tell me what happened. He was standing next to me but his voice seemed a long way off, fractured and disconnected. David had not turned up for an important work meeting. A colleague went to check whether his car was parked in the usual place. It was, but with David slumped across the steering wheel.

Lifeless.

Chapter 2

The next few months passed in a blur with me, the outsider, looking on enviously as everyone else carried on as normal. Friends and relatives told me how well I was doing, how strong I was being for Amy. As things stood, if it hadn't been for my daughter I'd have tried to find a way to join David wherever he was. Amy's way of coping was to retreat to her bedroom, spending hours listening to music. Not her own favourite music. Instead she played David's albums over and over. The very music she used to hate – 'saddo rock' – was now her direct link to dad. Sometimes the familiar tunes were a comfort and for a few hours it would feel like he was still here. Other times they would cut into my memories, clawing, burning into my head and I'd flee the house to escape the torment.

Three years on and it's time to move away, to start afresh. The house is far too big and I feel lost inside it. Without David and Amy to look after, I need a something to distract myself. So it's project 'down size' and I've seen a couple of smaller houses in need of an update. A bit like yours truly… *'lol'* as Amy would write in her text speak.

So back to conquering this lifelong fear of heights. If I'm honest, it's not just the original recipe book I'm keen to get my hands on. There's something else up there that I've been thinking about a lot for several days. Thoughts from the distant past stirred up by the recent headlines and that damn radio chat show. The gaggle of aging celebrities being arrested and questioned by the police, childhood heroes shattered. Accusations, denials, endless talk about 'sexual mores' of the 1970s and 80s. Calls for inquiries and apologies for past wrongs. Promises that it won't happen again.

The stuff of moral panic.

Then the phone call I received the other day. The one that has shaken my world and has left me unable to sleep properly, my brain in a kind of permanent jet lag state. Not the ideal state for confronting a major phobia but it's now or never.

My legs are jelly-like as I begin to climb up the rickety loft ladder. 'Don't look down' I whisper. One shaky step at a time. Go on, you can do it.

It takes me a few minutes to find the light switch and my heart is pounding so fast that I begin to feel dizzy. It's a relief to get some light onto the place and slowly I start to drink in the scene. Multi coloured plastic boxes, each neatly stacked and labelled in David's familiar spidery handwriting. Gaps, like missing teeth, where Amy has removed his stash of vinyl and CDs. My heart stops for a moment when I spot David's old work overalls.

Paint splattered and well worn, they might still smell of him.

I hold them to my face and take some deep breaths. Tears seep into the faded cloth as I crouch on the dusty floor, not wanting to let go of that last remnant of David. Yet let go I must. Remember, a new start.

My eyes are drawn to a small pile stacked up against the left corner wall. Some garishly covered exercise books with childish felt tip doodles all over them, a pile of yellowing Jackie magazines, some rolled up exam certificates and the fading red cover of my granny's recipe book.

Then I spot the diary, buried inside its pink patent cover. My name is written on the front in silver glittery ink. 'Debs 1975'. The rusting lock on the front, its key long disappeared. Amazingly that lock has stayed intact for decades, the keeper of teenage dreams and secrets.

Scooping up the mementoes of my former life into a discarded plastic bag, I feel an overwhelming need to escape – the heat is oppressive and rivulets of sweat are running down my face. Mixed with tears, a briny brew of sadness and panic. I make my way gingerly down the ladder, legs trembling with each step.

Still I've finally done it and I can hear David teasing me. 'Well done scaredy cat, now leave my man cave alone.' I wish.

After a long walk to clear my head, it's time to return to the stash rescued from the loft. Amy will soon have granny's battered recipe book but not before one last browse, tracing the outline of her impeccable handwriting with my fingers. I can taste each dish and can see her birdlike figure hunched over a mixing bowl with me looking on in awe. Some pages are splattered with buttery fingerprints and dried out bits of baking mix. For a while I'm transported to a tiny kitchen in inner city Birmingham, with an old record player blasting out wartime tunes.

'They don't write them like that any more Deborah' she'd say, refusing to use my shortened name. However many times I reminded her that I hated being called 'Deborah', she'd just ignore me and carry on regardless. That was granny for you. Stubborn like me.

The light is fading as I pour myself a large glass of Merlot and after a few cack-handed stabs with a paper knife, the diary finally pops open. A faded photo booth picture flutters down onto the floor. Me, aged 15, with my best mate Charlotte or 'Charlie' as she liked to call herself, after our favourite perfume of the time. The date on the back says January 11 1975. That explains the heavy winter coats and scarves. We're both pulling silly faces but I can see that we've made a stupendous effort with our make-up. Loads of shiny lip gloss and heavy duty mascara. Me, with long dark curly hair, teased out to look fuller. Charlie's blond hair wispier and unevenly layered.

Immediately I'm back to Saturday shopping in the city centre, followed by lingering coffees and cake in the market café. We look so ridiculously young, which of course we were, but I know we spent hours getting ready for those shopping trips. The idea was to look like we're 18 and preferably more like 21. The older the better – unlike now where I spend a fortune on lotions and potions trying to look younger. The irony.

At the time we lived in Hampton, a tiny Warwickshire commuter village, which for a teenager was pure hell. Zippo to do and no decent boys to chat up. The shopping trips and our weekly night out at the Long Room nightclub in a seedier part of Birmingham, saved us from dying of boredom.

Funny how you can be friends with someone for years and then just lose contact. I wonder what Charlie is doing right now? We lost touch when I moved to Cornwall just a year after that photo was taken. Wrenched viciously apart in the summer of 1975.

A summer that changed everything. Forever.

Chapter 3

My 1975 diary begins innocuously enough with the usual moans about school work, not being able to go out during the week, mum Christine and dad Alan being the 'worst parents in the whole wide world', not to mention that brat of a sister, 9 year old Carol. Too young to be interesting but old enough to be a pain in the arse. All recorded in different shades of ink with the giant multi coloured biro Charlie had bought me the previous Christmas.

There are fantasy plans, outlined in gushing teen speak, for me and Charlie to run away to London and blag our way into glamorous jobs in fashion. Or a glossy magazine. Or perhaps a record store or even a studio. The plans varied from day to day but we never waivered about London. Anything other than staying put and doing the summer job at the local council my mum was trying to fix up for me.

Then the glorious sense of freedom when my last exam is over.

'Yippee - final exam today! Never want to do another one in my life. Me and Charlie got tipsy on cider pinched from her dad's garage. Sick when I got home but still a

happy day. Start of the rest of my life - London here we come!'

I celebrate by buying the shortest purple dress I can find and matching suede wedge platform shoes. I'm already 5 foot 8 inches tall and most of it is leg. The legs are my best feature and I'm determined to make the most of them.

I can sense my excitement in the entry for Friday 25 July.

'Me and Charlie tried on our outfits for tomorrow night. She's got a great bright red midi skirt and white lacy top but I'm sticking to a mini and think my choice is loads better. Mum and dad are whingeing that it's too short the boring old farts. Can't believe that I've finally managed to get tickets for Mr DJ's Smokin' Hot disco at the Long Room. The place will be packed and we're getting there early to bag a place near the stage. One more night to go.'

Mr DJ's Smokin' Hot disco. The name sounds so corny now, pathetic really. Yet for a 15 - going on 16 - girl of the mid-70s, those words were the height of sophistication. A glimpse into the grown up world of great music, rebellion and excitement. The only place to be.

Then there was Mr DJ, legend in his own right and publicity machine. A god-like figure with a fan club of teenage girls, all hoping to catch his eye. He had a mop of dark curly hair and the lanky look of Phil Lynott from the group Thin Lizzy. Except Mr

DJ, (real name Pete Davis), was a sharper dresser and the music he played a world away from rock. He was into disco, soul, reggae. Dance music loved especially by the girls who would scream when he shouted out his catch phrase 'Up on the floor or out the door!'

The queues started at 8.00pm even though the doors didn't open until 10.00pm. It was ticket only and the gaggle of girls, some with boyfriends but most of them without, would get more loud and excitable as they waited for the doors to be flung open. Usually me and Charlie could only look on enviously, wishing we had one of the magic tickets. Not tonight though.

For the first time we were in with the coolest kids in town. Kids who couldn't wait to jump into the forbidden world of adulthood.

Chapter 4

Looking back now, I wonder what would have happened if mum and dad had got their way and stopped me from going out that night.

'You look like a bloody street walker'. Dad was furious when I emerged from the bedroom, a vision in purple. 'Get changed into something decent.'

Stung by the venom in his voice, I darted back into the bedroom. I could hear him yelling for mum who was out in the back garden getting in some washing. This was my one and only chance. Within seconds I was tearing down the road towards the bus stop. Charlie was already there waiting and for once the bus was on time. As I looked out of the back window, I could see mum and dad careering around the corner. Charlie and me couldn't stop laughing all the way to town.

Still, if they had succeeded…

A few hours after I fled the house, there I was standing just inches from this Adonis of the night club. Mr mesmerising. Mr sex on legs. Mr DJ himself. Charlie and me had sneaked some vodka into old perfume bottles and were well tiddly by the time we got to the club. We swore to the doorman that we were 18 and at work. No ID needed in those days and we certainly looked the part. I blushed as the doorman said I had 'a great pair of pins on me'. Of course I knew it but it was nice to get the affirmation.

Then the moment when I caught the eye of Mr DJ. Charlie had gone to the loo to apply more industrial strength make up and I was guarding our drinks, bought at the bar this time, at extortionate night club prices.

I looked up to see him beckoning me up to the stage. Yes me, being summoned by the great man. Where the hell was Charlie to witness this earth shattering event? Out of the frame for the sake of some sodding make up.

My diary comes to an abrupt halt after that momentous night, the last time I ever kept one. Funny to think of that now. I was just a month away from my sixteenth birthday and about to fulfil that ambition to leave home. Never did get to buy that fantasy flat near the Kings Road with Charlie. No, my new place was a whole lot different and as far down South as you can get before hitting the Atlantic Ocean.

But back to Mr DJ. By the time Charlie returned from the loo, I was up on stage and the envy of every girl in the place.

'Go on, pick your favourite slow record' he

whispered as he wrapped his arm around my waist. I could smell his musky aftershave and giggled as he told me that I was the most gorgeous girl in the place.

'Legs right up to your armpits' he added as he put on some track that he ended up choosing. Don't ask me what it was. Next I remember being swept onto the dance floor and Charlie grinning away in the background. Ecstatic doesn't do it justice.

'Wait for me afterwards' he whispered as he leapt back onto the stage.

And wait I did. It was gone 3am before he'd packed up all his gear and crammed it into his tatty white van. An hour before, I'd told Charlie to get her taxi home. We both knew what was going to happen and I promised to tell her all about it tomorrow. I can still remember my last words to her.

'Sort out mum and dad. I'll ring tomorrow morning so we can get our story right.'

'Be careful' she replied.

Truth be told, I don't remember much about losing my virginity. It was all over so quickly and we spent the rest of the night sleeping in the back of the smelly van. Well he slept. I spent most of the night staring at him, imagining how jealous the other girls would be when they got to hear about this and wondering how to tell Charlie that sex really wasn't all it was cracked up to be. The next morning we had another hurried session before Mr DJ had to get going to prepare for his next gig up in Liverpool. Charlie came up with a story about me staying the night over at her place because I was too scared to go home. Mum and dad were so relieved to see me back safely that they didn't say too much. But dad kept giving me disapproving glares and I'm pretty sure mum suspected something too.

Our 'relationship' if you can call it that, only lasted for another three weeks. At least the sex did get better and we had use of his tiny bedsit in leafy Edgbaston, where I visited most weekday afternoons.

And then it was all over, almost as quickly as it began, with Mr DJ announcing that he was heading North where the club scene was 'hotting up' big time. It really was as brutal and simple as that.

Me? As it turned out, mum and dad were actually quite pleased when I announced out of the blue that I'd got the chance of a summer job at a hotel in Cornwall. It would get me away from the influence of 'that Charlie', they said. If only they knew.

A sex abuse victim? Isn't that what everyone is now saying? After all, he was the older guy who should have known better and I was a naïve teenager. Best to keep things simple, the innocent and perpetrator.

Well he didn't ask my age and neither did I own

up. He was a hunter, a predator as they'd say today, but no-one can tell me that I didn't want it to happen.

And yet....

I watch as the smoke rises from the pyre of my former life. Pink molten plastic from my diary cover seeping into David's smouldering blue overalls.

My hand is shaking as I reach across to my laptop computer, typing in 'Mr DJ' and 'Pete Davis' into the search engine.

The start of a journey. One to who knows where.

Chapter 5

It doesn't take long to track down an address for Pete Davis, aka Mr DJ. After just a few minutes of searching and I have an address in Beaconsfield, Buckinghamshire. Then there are all the press reports mentioning Peter Davis – he has reverted to his full name – the 'music mogul' and celebrity big wig. Pictures show a grey haired bespectacled pin-striped business type, still whippet thin and still recognisably the Mr DJ of the past. The eyes are exactly the same, deep brown and piercing. The years have served him well.

I'm shocked to read that he is now in his early 70s, a lot older than I thought. It means that he must have been at least 35 years old in the summer of 1975. So not quite the young DJ in his mid 20s that I'd been led to believe. But then, as I well know, he wasn't the only one lying through his teeth about his age.

According to one report from a few years ago, he is divorced from his second wife and she has got custody of their two young sons. Another article mentions a grown up daughter from his first marriage.

The press pieces seem to have tailed off recently, so it's difficult to know whether he's still working. A quick look on Street View shows that he lives in the sort of road that doesn't permit camera shots – no sneak preview of his house allowed. A road that yells expensive and exclusive. A world way then from the scruffy white van stinking of cigarettes, sweat and god knows what else.

Still, I have an address and that's all that matters for now. I've been so engrossed in my search for Mr DJ that I haven't even noticed the light flashing on my mobile phone. It's from Amy, the queen of text communication, who will only usually ring in a 'dire' emergency - in other words, when she needs her bank account topping up or something 'urgent' posted off that she has managed to leave behind in the rush to pack for 'uni'. Ugh, when did the lovely word university get so horribly truncated?

'Mum – did you remember that recipe I mentioned the other day? Just text me with what I need to buy to make about 12. I assume they can be frozen? BTW, how is the house move going? Love you oodles. Xx'

I reply by jotting down the details and telling her to keep an eye out for granny's recipe book in the post, adding jauntily that *'I expect you to become an ace cook – it's in the genes you know!'*

Her reply makes me smile.

'Mum I didn't expect you to answer so quickly – it's 2.30am. Why are you still up? I thought you'd gone to

bed ages ago. I've got an essay to finish, so I've got no choice. Now get to bed! Xxx'

Actually I haven't noticed the time and Amy's right – I've got work to go to in the next few hours and a couple are coming back for a second house viewing in the afternoon. So I'll need to do a tidy up and make sure there's some fresh coffee brewing. Yes, I've read all those house selling books, the ones that say uber cleaning, flowers and that all important coffee pot really do work their magic. Truth is I'm terrified that this couple will actually like what they see and put in an offer. Then it will be really happening, chez McKay will be getting new owners and I'll be moving on to the next stage of my life. Starting with a different address on the other side of town.

The alarm wrenches me from a deep sleep and a dream that David is still alive. We are shopping in central Truro and trying to remember where we've parked the car. I'm frantic with worry because we have left a much younger Amy there reading her book, while David is being his usual laid back and infuriating self. It is a classic anxiety dream involving search and panic. I can feel the sweat running down my back as I take some deep breaths to calm myself. Then the feeling of overwhelmingly emptiness as I realise that David is not here with me and never will be again.

Work for me is a part-time job as a lifestyle feature writer for Cornwall Now, a glossy coffee table magazine appealing to both visitors and aspirational locals. 'Back in the day' as they say, I began my working life as a reporter on the Cornish Echo, a weekly newspaper, but after Amy was born I decided that I needed something more child friendly. Nineteen years on and I'm still at Cornwall Now, doing the same job after turning down several offers to take on a more senior editorial role. Managing people never did appeal and with David then travelling all over the country in his role as a company sales rep, I wanted Amy to have at least one parent at home when she got back from school. I didn't see it as a lack of ambition but more about providing consistency for Amy. And as my own mum was forever reminding me, we 'didn't need the money.'

'Morning Debbie... the usual is it?'

I'm standing, still half asleep, in Dave's Café just across the road from the Cornwall Now office. Cathy, the young waitress, is poised by the Expresso machine, ready to serve my essential morning pick-me-up.

'Make it a large one today,' I reply 'and throw in one of those blueberry muffins while you're at it.'

Cathy smiles knowingly.

'Need some extra energy today? Hard night was it eh?'

I mutter something about wanting to keep awake for a dull work meeting and inwardly curse as the darkened skies suddenly turn into torrential rain.

'Shit – I haven't got my brolly' I mumble as Cathy passes over my order.

'Here, take mine' she says reaching behind the counter and handing over an enormous bright yellow golfing style umbrella. 'Just drop it back over on your way home.'

As if I'd want to keep the monstrosity. I'm struggling to shake the water off my jumbo advertisement for Cornwall's 'best spa experience' – who writes this stuff? – when Kevin Foster, the magazine Sub Editor, hurtles through the door, his drenched hair stuck to his head and shirt looking like it has missed out on the drying cycle in a washing machine.

'Jeez – what a piss down. Got like this just walking from the car. Christ, where did you get that brolly? Must be visible from outer space.'

' Nothing to do with me – it's Cathy's from over the road. So spill the beans Kevin. What's this meeting all about?'

I'd had an odd sounding email yesterday afternoon from Elaine Mason, Cornwall Now's Managing Editor. It was a bit vague, just something about a 'general meeting' at 9am and that she wanted everybody there.

'You haven't heard the rumours then?' Kevin replies, trying haplessly to stem the drips from his sodden clothes.

I have no idea what he's talking about and it shows.

'Well share some of that gorgeous smelling coffee of yours and I'll fill you in.'

Somehow I sense it isn't going to be good news as I follow Kevin into his messy cubby hole of an office.

Not good at all.

Chapter 6

I just about make it back in time to meet Jane and Alex, the young couple coming for a second look at my house. Forget extra cleaning, a smell of coffee will have to do. Damn it, there is even a strategically placed vase of fresh flowers on the kitchen table and given what I've just gone through this morning, they are lucky to get that.

Mercifully they don't stay long.

'It's a beautiful house Mrs McKay' Jane says looking across at her husband for confirmation. 'Really gorgeous, you must be sorry to leave it.'

'Call me Debbie' I reply trying to size up whether her comment is genuine or just an attempt to be polite. I decide that she probably does mean it but Alex isn't giving too much away. A man with a beady eye on the price negotiation.

'We'll have another chat and get back to you later' Jane says as they head back to their car.

'Take your time, it's a big decision' I reply using the psychology advice from my latest house selling manual. Go for the soft approach and don't make it look like you are desperate. Imply that there might be other interested parties waiting.

It's only 3pm but I already feel like a stiff drink. I've always felt uncomfortable about drinking alcohol in the middle of the afternoon, especially if I'm alone, and it took a shed load of will power not to hit the bottle in the months after David died. But sod it, today I'm going to make an exception.

I'm already on my second large gin when the doorbell chimes loudly. Surely it's not my would-be house buyers returning already?

Shoving my drink in the fridge, I make a dash to the door, hoping that my breath doesn't reek of booze. I can see through the stained glass window – one of the 'original features' buyers love – that it's Kevin the Sub Editor.

'Hi Debbie – I was just driving past and thought I'd pop in to see how you are.'

I spot the bottle of wine jutting out of his supermarket carrier bag. Another poor soul in need of self medication.

Actually I'm quite pleased to see him. Kevin is always good company even in a crisis and it will be good to get his early take on this morning's bizarre meeting. He'd been right to warn me earlier that there were job redundancies looming.

After rescuing my own drink and pouring him a large glass of his own expensive South African red – 'you're pushing the boat out Kevin'- we head into the conservatory to get some late afternoon sun.

'So what did you think then?' he says after a few minutes of taking in the garden view. It's one of the many things I will really miss about this house.

I pause for a moment before replying. After all, I'm in a different situation from most people on Cornwall Now. Mortgage paid off, a hefty sum left from life insurance and David's pension. I carry on working because I want to, not out of financial necessity. Unlike Kevin who has a family to keep and massive out goings.

'Well I'm glad you tipped me off about what was coming. I honestly had no idea. That's the trouble about working part-time, you get disconnected and out of the loop.'

I notice how he has managed to get through most of his glass of wine in two large gulps. Poor guy must be worried sick.

'The rumours really started a few weeks ago,' he says reaching over to top up his drink. 'The writing has been on the wall for months though. All that nit picking over expenses, not sending people to cover big events, cutting corners on production. Yep, could see it coming but still...' His stops to take another large swig and I mentally make a note to get us something to eat soon. I'll also make sure he leaves his car here even if I have to pay for his taxi home.

Two hours on and I've just sent a well oiled

Kevin off, his battered estate car still sitting on my drive. Despite the grim news about job losses on the magazine, it's been good to have some company. I've done my best to reassure him that decent Sub Editors are in demand and that they are bound to hang on to him, even in the new 'leaner and meaner' regime. I don't think I've succeeded though and it looks like he is already applying for other jobs outside Cornwall. As for me, well I know that I'm likely to be given the big heave-ho. I like to think of myself as a decent feature writer but I'm aware that there are an army of interns willing to work for nothing to get their first big break. Experience over cheapness? I'm pretty sure which one is going to win.

Now I've got rid of Kevin, it is crunch time. After tracking down an address for Mr DJ – I'm going to carry on calling him that – should I go ahead and write to him? After all, he was the first man I had sex with and with all this stuff in the news, there are a few things preying on my mind.

Not least the troubling phone call but much more about that later.

Of course he won't remember me and I know I was just one in a long line of girls. Still, he was a fleeting but important figure in my teenage life.

Compared to Amy, who is always taking photos of herself and posting them on social networking sites, I have very few pictures of myself from the time I met Mr DJ. Just the faded photo booth one of me and my best mate clowning around, some school photos in my hideous bottle green uniform and another of me looking miserable at my 16th birthday meal. Mum and dad are on there trying to look cheerful, while little sis Carol is busy stuffing her face. Even though I don't have happy memories of the evening, I feel wistful looking at this snapshot in time. Dad looking dapper in his best brown suit and tie, while mum is wearing a loud floral dress with a fussy neck bow. They are only in their early forties but look much older. Dad died over ten years ago and mum now lives a long way off with Carol and her family in Wales. Given that I'm likely to be made redundant any day soon, I might have a bit more time to visit.

Let's wait and see.

So, assuming I'm going to take the plunge and contact Mr DJ, I'll need to choose which picture to send. The smiley mucking around one, or the miserable cow? If I scan in the one from the photo booth into my computer, I can always get Kevin to play around with it and take out Charlie. He'll also be able to improve the colour, focus more on my face and big mid-70s hair do. Trouble is I'm pulling a stupid face and it doesn't make sense without Charlie in the picture. So she'll need to stay whether I like it or not.

One thing I've already decided on if I do get in touch - it's got to be a hand written letter. No emails or phone calls, not to start with. I like the idea of old fashioned letters, it sort of fits in with the memories of a time long before the internet and mobile phones. A time when hand written letters and notes were the norm and phone calls were made from those old red call boxes, usually stinking of piss and vomit. I've even dug out some long forgotten stationery, a Christmas present from mum and never used. Not yet anyway.

Right - time to stop the procrastinating. To write or not to write? I remember how dad used to throw a coin whenever he had a tricky choice to make. So it's 'heads' to get writing and 'tails' to forget all about it. I dig out a coin from my purse and flick it high into the air, covering my eyes so that I can't see it fall. It lands with a dull thud on the oak floor.

Slowly I move my fingers apart, peering down through my splayed fingers.

And the coin has landed head side up.

Chapter 7

So two whole months have flown by since my 'flick of the coin' decision to make contact with Mr DJ and a lot has happened in that time.

The couple who came for the second viewing of the house decided to buy it. A lower offer than I expected but not a silly one. Now everything is packed up ready for my move ten miles down the road towards the centre of Truro. My new home is an Edwardian semi and, as the estate agent says, 'in need of a complete update'. For that read 'massive make-over.' It does have a tiny walled garden which also requires some serious TLC. When Amy first saw the place she said it was 'cute, like an old fashioned doll's house.' She has a point.

Amy has promised to help me do it up during her long summer break but I'm not holding my breath. A few of her friends are heading off to work on an American kids summer camp and Amy has dropped hints that she'd like to go. Actually I'd like her to go as well because then I can crack on with my blank canvas decorating, without having to tip toe around a moody 19 year old. Especially one wishing she was thousands of miles away with her mates.

The news on the work front isn't as bad as I thought. Yes, I've been made redundant but there's an offer of regular freelance contributions and even the possibility of a monthly column. Kevin Foster has managed to hang on to his job too, so at least he can pay the mortgage and keep his son at a small but expensive private school in Truro. There's the added bonus that I still have my good drinking pal to put the world to rights with.

By and large then, all is well with my world. Now the house move is getting closer, I have no more excuses to put off writing that letter to Mr DJ. A quick check with the electoral register shows he is still living in Beaconsfield and there has even been a recent newspaper photo of him at a local fete. He looks very much the picture of a prosperous local businessman, expensive looking linen jacket and jaunty straw sun hat. He's standing beside one of those old style 'juke box' pub record players – the sort that has vinyl singles inside – and the caption says that it is one of his prized vintage collection. He's the picture of upper middle class respectability these days, with straighter and whiter teeth than I remember too.

So, how to begin the letter? I'm a writer by trade and you'd think it would be easy. If only. In the early hours of this morning, I lay awake thinking that I must be mad to get back in touch. Do I really believe that he'll remember some ditzy girl from the mid-70s, just one of the many to fall for this Lothario of the club scene? Am I turning into some crazy middle-aged bint?

I've got to start somewhere so here goes. I'll take things gently to begin with, using the house move as the excuse for getting in touch. Everyone knows that a move means going through old photos and memorabilia. You know the score – 'hey, I just saw this photo from back in the day and it reminded me of you'. Corny but handy. For writing purposes I'll use his full name, rather than the Mr DJ one.

Dear Peter,

I hope you don't mind me contacting you after all these years. I'm enclosing a photo of me back in the summer of 1975 when we first met. I was Debs 'Clark' back then and you were still known locally as 'Mr DJ' with a regular spot at the Long Room nightclub in Birmingham.

I'm about to move house – I now live in deepest Cornwall – and going through my old stuff has brought the memories flooding back. I did a quick computer search and managed to track down an address for you. It might seem strange that I've decided to hand write this letter but it is so much more elegant than e-mail, don't you think? Just the physical act of hand writing, takes me back in time.

A lot has happened to me over the years and I know, (at least from what I've read), the same is true of you. Not long after you went off to explore the club scene in Manchester, I headed in the other direction down to

Cornwall. I suppose I just wanted to get as far away as possible and I've always had this thing about living by the sea. Having tasted the world of grown ups – all those times in your little bedsit opposite the cricket ground in Edgbaston! – I needed to move on, to get some independence. So I got a job as a trainee receptionist at a small seaside hotel, living on the premises.

The job was fine for a while but I knew that it wasn't what I wanted to do longer term. I'd managed to squirrel away a fair amount of money and enrolled on a journalism course before moving to Truro to work on a weekly newspaper. That's when I met my husband, David, who was working in the advertising department. We set up house together and had a daughter, Amy. She's now 19 and at university in Bristol studying English. Sadly, David passed away a couple of years ago only a few months after his 50th birthday. He had a massive stroke and died instantly, so mercifully he didn't have a long drawn out illness. Of course it was a terrible time and a huge shock. I thought I'd go mad with grief but somehow managed to get through things and had to be strong for Amy.

I'm now working as a freelance magazine writer and about to embark on the next stage of my life, wherever it takes me. When I was clearing out my loft, I came across a diary from 1975 and found the photo of me at the time with my best friend Charlie. (She used to cover for me when I went to meet you). So here I am, literally putting pen to paper, hoping that we can correspond in this way for old time's sake. I'd love to hear more about your life and what you are doing now. I'm deliberately not *including a phone number or email because I'd really like you just to write back. I remember that you had neat hand writing for a bloke, though that could have changed after all this time! Look forward to your reply and I've put my new home address as I'll be living there by the time you get this letter. Back to the last minute packing....*

All the best,

Debbie McKay

If this was a magazine piece, I'd put it aside as a first draft and re-read it the next morning. Nine times out of ten, I'd change a few things and add extra thoughts. Not tonight though. I know if I don't post it off, I'll risk another change of heart.

The letter plops into the empty sounding post box and now there's no going back.

What's done is done.

Chapter 8

The new house is starting to grow on me but still feels strange, like sneaking around somebody else's place. There is a stubborn whiff of cigar smoke which keeps hanging around, despite my efforts with scented candles and perfumed room sprays. Of course, the answer is to crack on with the decorating because the smell of paint always cancels out other things. But somehow I can't summon up the energy to start the home renovations just yet. I need to get a sense of the place, a feel for the rooms and what colours will work where. This is going to be my place, a home to fit the new singleton lifestyle. As I keep telling myself, there's no need to rush.

My next door neighbour is a sprightly 85 year-old gent called Ted and he has already offered to help me out with getting the garden in shape. I feel that it's me who should be offering help, though he's probably the fitter one from the look of him. Ted is also a widower but has a gaggle of 'lady friends' as he puts it.

'Need to keep all options open at my age' he says, giving me a cheeky wink. Perhaps I'll decline that offer of help, just in case I'm being sized up to join Ted's harem. When I tell Amy this she bursts out laughing.

'Yuk, mum - as if. You're much too glamorous for that old codger. What about that friend of yours, that guy Kevin? He's quite sexy for a middle-aged man.'

We're speaking via Skype so that we can see each other. Amy has her hair in bendy curlers, in readiness for her planned girls' night out. Even in this state, she looks gorgeous and has inherited David's blonde good looks.

'Kevin's already spoken for,' I remind her. 'Anyway, never mind me. When am I going to meet this Ashley bloke you've been talking about?'

Despite her striking looks, Amy has had surprisingly few of what I'd call 'proper boyfriends'. There was one called Mitch when she was in sixth form college, a lanky serious type who was into Goth fashion and wore more black eye liner than Amy. Then there was a brief holiday fling in Portugal which inevitably fizzled out once we got back to England. Ha, so much for those optimistic youthful promises to 'keep in touch'.

'Now mum, you'll meet him soon enough. It is early days and I'm still not sure about him. I've got to admit he's good looking though and has a great sense of humour.'

I can see her fiddling with the hair rollers which is Amy speak for 'shut up mum, I need to go and get ready.'

'All right but if it does get beyond the wild sex stage, bring him down to Truro for the weekend. He sounds nice.'

Even on the Skype screen, I can see Amy's face reddening.

'Ugh mum – enough, *please*. Listen, I've got to go now but I'll see you next weekend. Bye then, love you.'

She blows a kiss which I return, inwardly cursing myself for embarrassing her. Who wants to hear their middle-aged mum talking about wild sex? No wonder she went scuttling off like that, poor thing.

I'm meeting Kevin Foster later for a drink and Amy is right – he is attractive in that swarthy Cornish sort of way. The pole opposite of David who could well have been a Scandanavian with his unruly mop of fair hair and tall muscular shape. Kevin is shorter and quite slim despite his love of real Cornish beer. He also has the palest of blue eyes, a notable contrast to his dark skin. But enough of that - as I've just reminded Amy, Kevin is happily married with two young boys. He's told me his wife knows all about our friendship and has no problem with him meeting me for a drink from time to time. Perhaps she feels safe because I'm in my early fifties, a good decade older than her and Kevin. I know I wouldn't have felt comfortable if David had another woman as a regular drinking buddy, older or not, which I suppose says a lot about my own insecurities.

Still, it's good to have an excuse for a non committal flirt and to make an effort with some eye shadow and lippy. Otherwise I'd be slopping around in my PJs with a TV dinner, feeling sorry for myself. A sad way to spend a Saturday night and as I know only too well, life is too short to waste time slumped on the sofa.

It's been nearly a month since I posted off my letter to Mr DJ and still no reply. And yes, hand on heart I'm disappointed. After all the inner angst about whether or not to get in touch, it was a relief to write the letter and get it sent off. I didn't expect an answer straight away but four weeks on and it's starting to feel like he isn't going to respond.

I want to confide in Kevin, to tell him about Mr DJ. Well, at least some of the carefully chosen edited highlights. When I arrive in our favourite pub, just a short walk away from my new home, he's already there clutching a beer and there's a large glass of Pinot Grigio on the table.

'Hey Debbie – you look glam tonight. The new hair style suits you.'

Good old Kevin, always making people feel fabulous. Actually, I'm pleased with my newer shorter hairstyle which I think suits my high cheekbones and rounded face. I've also gone for some gold high lights to perk up my naturally brown hair and to disguise the white streaks which have started to appear. I'm wearing a tight red dress to show off my newly slimmed down figure. After David's death, I shed two stones without trying and have managed to lose even more weight with the stress of moving house. Yes, I think I look pretty damn good for my age and smile back at Kevin appreciatively.

'Well, I've just got off a Skype phone call to my beautiful daughter so it's nice to get a compliment' I say, sliding into my seat and raising my wine glass at Kevin.

Three glasses of wine later and I think I'm ready to involve him in my decision to contact Mr DJ.

'Right then Kevin, can I trust you not to say a word to anybody else if I share something with you? You have to promise.'

He stares back at me with the inquisitive eyes of the journalist that he is.

'Of course you can trust me. You don't have to ask – come on Debbie, how long have we known each other now? '

'Ten years to be exact. But I still need you to promise.'

'Bloody hell Debbie. Of course I promise. You're not in any trouble are you?'

'No, of course not. Tell you what, buy me another drink and I'll put you out of your misery.'

'A large one?' His eyes are twinkling in anticipation of a good story or bit of gossip.

'Yep and let's order bar snacks while you're at it.'

It's going to be a long night and I'll need to do some serious story tweaking to bypass Kevin's supreme editor's nose.

Make sure that he doesn't manage to read too much between the lines.

Chapter 9

'Quills' pub is starting to fill up with the usual Saturday night mix of twenty somethings on their way to a Club and everyone else in between. That's why I like this place, it's a drinking den that is hard to define. A microcosm of the city itself.

'So come on then, spill it out' Kevin says, dipping a chunk of crusty bread – or 'artisan rustic' as it says on the menu – into a small bowl of olive oil.

'You mustn't laugh Kevin. I've really given this some thought you know.'

'Bloody hell Debbie. Are you going to tell me or what?' He has a small slick of oil on his chin which I gesture towards and pass him a paper napkin.

'I wrote a letter a few weeks ago to someone I haven't seen in nearly forty years.'

'Eh – did I hear right. A letter?' He finishes dabbing his chin, feeling around for any bits he might have missed.

'You're fine now Kevin. Yes, a letter and I mean a proper hand written one.'

He raises an eyebrow and swallows his chunk of

bread.

'Blimey, I haven't hand written anything for years – bloody decades. I doubt whether I could do it any more. Why pen and paper anyway?'

'Just because it felt right – very, you know, 1975. That's when I last saw him.'

'So it's a '*him*' then?' Kevin dunks another piece of bread and passes the slate platter over to me. Slate plates seem to be the trendy thing these days, with everything served up on them. They seem to be the equivalent of food in a basket served up in 1970s pubs. I've lost my appetite and push it back towards Kevin. He shrugs and helps himself to a chunk of cheese. Artisan and local of course.

'Yes a him, and a much *older* him as it happens.' He glances up, suddenly more interested.

'Well at the time I thought he was in his twenties but I've been doing some digging and it turns out he was in his mid thirties at the time. He was my first proper boyfriend back in the Midlands.'

Kevin stares back at me and I can see he's trying to do some quick age calculations. I put him out of his misery.

'I was 15 at the time, going on 16 actually. He was a hot shot local DJ called Pete Davis. Everyone called him Mr DJ though.'

Kevin snorts derisively at the mention of the moniker 'Mr DJ'.

'Bloody hell Debbie – he was old enough to be your dad. Your first *"boyfriend"* you say?' I can already sense the disapproval, even though he is trying hard to conceal it behind the distraction technique of taking a large gulp of beer.

'Don't forget, I *thought* he was 25 and before you say anything, I lied to him about my age as well. I told him I was 19 and I looked the part too.'

Kevin leans across the table and lowers his voice.

'When you say he was your first boyfriend, I'm assuming….?'

'He was the first person I had sex with if that's what you mean' I reply and Kevin instinctively turns around to see if anyone is listening. Of course they aren't.

'Whoa, too much information. Sorry Debbie but I can't pretend to like the idea of a guy in his thirties, even in his twenties, sleeping with a girl of 15. Still, I suppose I shouldn't be surprised with all this celebrity stuff in the news.' He takes another drink, more slowly this time.

'I hadn't put you down as the moral crusader type' I say, miffed by his willingness to condemn before he's heard the full story. Well, as much of it I'm prepared to divulge.

'OK, putting the age thing aside, why get in touch after all these years? He has to be in his 70s now, probably a grandad too.'

I've got to be careful here. After several large glasses of wine, I need to keep my wits about me.

'I suppose it was going through all my old things before the house move. I found my diary from 1975 and it brought everything back. Anyway, it didn't take me long to track him down and I thought, why not?' I scan Kevin's face to see if he senses that I'm leaving something out but I don't get any clues.

'Hmm – I can think of a hundred "why nots". He could be a cantankerous old git, or his wife – if he has one – could be really pissed off. He could be a sad old drunk or druggie. You never know what you're getting into....'

A young woman in an uber short skirt brushes past us on her way to the bar and he stops mid rant. There's a sideways eye flicker but he manages to avoid the full on stare. I can't help smiling and he reddens slightly at being caught out.

'Come on Kevin, what sort of journalist do you think I am? I've done my research, remember? No, he isn't married anymore, he got divorced a few years ago. He's got two young boys under 10 from that marriage and an older daughter from a previous one. I've seen a recent photo and he looks pretty good for his age to me. '

Kevin helps himself to some more bread and dipping oil as he takes in this bit of information.

'Not a DJ anymore then?' The mini skirted girl walks past again clutching her drink. This time he makes an effort not to gawk.

I ignore his sarcasm.

'No, it seems he's been working as a music publicist and looks like he's made a mint. His house is in one of those gated communities and he collects vintage records and those old pub juke boxes.'

Kevin stares at me for a few moments longer than feels comfortable. I look away and grab my wine glass.

'You still haven't answered my question properly. Just why are you *really* contacting this guy? You can't still have feelings for him?'

Perceptive old Kevin. Yes, he does sense that there is more to this story than meets the eye.

'Nah, course not. It was a long time ago, another age. But I'm just curious that's all. Don't you ever wonder what has happened to your first girlfriend?'

Kevin stares at his nearly empty drink and shakes his head.

'Not for one minute. Her name was Mandy Rutter and she turned out to be a bloody nutter.' He laughs at the rhyming slang.

'Sounds like something Ian Dury would have written about. Now before I tell you more about Mr DJ, are you ready for a top up?'

Kevin gives me the thumbs up and as I make my way to the bar, the girl in the short skirt gives me a smile. I realise that her outfit could have come straight out of the 1970s and it would have been my choice of Saturday night gear way back then.

And I can't help wondering if she is trying to do what I did all those years ago. Look a lot older and more sophisticated than she really is. Kevin is staring across in our direction and I know full well that his main attention is on the girl standing right next to me.

Time may have hurtled by but some things just don't change. Ever.

Chapter 10

I'm feeling quite tipsy by the time I get home and make myself some tea and toast to mop up the alcohol. Kevin's reaction to my contacting Mr DJ has more than pissed me off but at least I've shared my news with someone.

I suppose I shouldn't be that surprised that he doesn't 'get' my need to reconnect with my past. He just sees it as one of those murky passages of adolescence, best forgotten. To cap it all, he even hinted that it could be a delayed reaction to grief over David, made worse by empty nest syndrome.

The one thing I'm sure about is that he's wrong on both counts. Of course I still miss David like crazy and it's not the same talking to Amy via a computer link. But at least I can see her when we do chat and she comes back home every third weekend or so. No, my motivation goes deeper than Kevin's amateur psychological assessment. Much deeper.

I must have nodded off on the sofa because I awake with a jolt. Someone is banging on the door and the telly is still switched on.

I rake my hands through my hair and stumble

into the hallway. My head is throbbing and I have a mouth is as dry as 'a badger's arse', to use one of David's favourite sayings.

'Hang on. I'll be with you in a minute.'

My heart sinks as I see the outline of old Ted through the glass door. He's wearing the bulky overcoat that never seems to leave his back. Clearly taken aback by my dishevelled state, he has the grace not to make glib small talk.

'Oh sorry to disturb you Debbie. This stuff was delivered to me and the Postie has shoved it through the wrong door. Only noticed when I went through my mail just now.'

I grab the pile off him with a perfunctory 'thank you'. Mercifully, he gets the none too subtle hint that I'm in no mood to talk further. It looks like it's a load of the usual junk mail and bills so time for a coffee before working my way through it. Whatever happened to the prediction of the paperless society?

A second large cup of coffee does the trick and I'm starting to feel human again. There's a piece to write up for Cornwall Now with a deadline for tomorrow afternoon. It's a restaurant review and I'll need to work around the fact that the place is overpriced and the food isn't much to write home about either. There's always a way of saying these things so that it doesn't sound too negative but I'll have to be in the right frame of mind. And Sunday morning with the residue of a hangover, isn't the time.

My eye catches a glimpse of a cream envelope buried beneath the pile of pizza offer flyers and brown paper bill demands. Could it be…? As I flick it sideways, it flutters to the floor and the handwriting is the giveaway.

Of course, it's from him.

I jump as the phone rings out. Jeez, talk about bad timing.

Snatching the receiver, my eyes are firmly fixed on that neat slanting written address. Delicate but bold at the same time. A confident hand.

Kevin sounds like he's just got out of bed.

'Hi Debbie – just checking you are OK. We both had a shed load of booze last night. Think I may have upset you with my big drunken mouth? ' He trails off, as if expecting an ear bashing.

'No, what's said in the pub, stays in the pub' I say lying through my teeth. Of course I'm still wracked off with him, irritated by his overwhelmingly negativity about my approach to Mr DJ.

He pauses for a moment, trying to read between the lines. Truth is, we know each other too well to bullshit and can pick up the tiniest of verbal clues.

'You sure? Well, if I did say something out of turn in drink then soz. You know what I'm like – a lightweight trying to keep up with the big boys. How's the head?'

'Better now I've had some strong coffee. Listen Kevin, it is sweet of you to call but I've got to dash. Old Ted from next door is due around any minute.' Another big fat whopper.

'OK, see you tomorrow then and make sure you get that review finished, hangover or not. And watch that Ted guy – you know what you're like with older men.'

Cheeky quip but I'm not getting into verbal banter just now. I still haven't taken my eyes off that letter, black ink on an expensive looking paper. I trace the lettering with my fingers and feel the silkiness of the finish. There is a feint smell, vanilla mixed with something else which I can't make out.

I take a couple of deep breaths before gently teasing the envelope open. More of that whiff of vanilla and if I'm not mistaken, a hint of cinnamon.

The letter inside is folded neatly and there is a small package covered in bubble wrap. I can feel my heart pounding as I carefully unfurl the paper. Oh well Debbie – here goes. The first communication in decades, mid-1970s crashing into the twenty-first century

'Dear Debbie,

I'm sorry for the delay in replying but I've been away on holiday in Florida and have just got back. What an

incredible and pleasant surprise to hear from you after all these years. Of course I remember you – the girl I first saw in the purple dress with the most amazing legs. How could I forget?

I love the idea of writing letters, what a great plan. I'm into a lot of vintage things these days and I'll tell you more about that at some point. Would you believe I'm writing this with a fountain pen which belonged to my grandad?! Now that's a real antique believe me.

Your photo brought everything back. They were such carefree days back then weren't they? I loved my 'Mr DJ' role and as you'll know – you're a journalist so I guess you have done your research – I stayed in the entertainment business, working on the publicity side. It was the best job ever, meeting all my music idols and going to some amazing gigs. I'm long retired now and spend my time trawling the antiques shops and auctions for music memorabilia, my new obsession.

Weren't you a budding fashion designer in those days? Or am I confusing you with someone else? I must confess that I was a typical 1970s macho male then, playing the field. But you always knew that, didn't you? You were a free spirit like me, wanting to grab the big wide world by the scruff of its neck. Funny though that you settled in Cornwall. I always had you down as a London bound girl, a real city chick.

I've been married and divorced twice, so I can't say I've been lucky in love. Still I've got three great kids out of it – twin boys, Freddie and Gene (named after two of my favourite musicians!) both just turned 10 and my oldest, Lulu, (guess who she's named after?!) is in her 30s now. I'm not a grandad yet but I suspect that will change sometime soon.

I'm sorry to hear about your husband dying at such a young age. It must be devastating to lose somebody so brutally like that but at least you have your daughter, who sounds like a clever girl.

Talking of clever, you've done well getting work on a glossy magazine. I looked it up online and read some of your articles. I haven't visited Cornwall in years and they make me want to go. Perhaps we could meet up there some time in the future? You look as attractive in your recent photos as you were back then, even prettier in some ways now you're not hiding behind that heavy 70s make up.

So how are we going to catch up after all this time? There is much to tell and to start with, I've enclosed some recent photos of me, my two boys and daughter. I also found a photo of me outside the bedsit in Edgbaston, taken about a year before we met. You'll see that time hasn't treated me quite as well as it has you – I've got a lot less hair now which is why I wear the hat most of the time. On the plus side, I haven't put on too much weight and the face is real – no surgery or lifts for me.

I'm so out of practice with real writing that my hand is starting to ache so I'll sign off for now. Look forward to hearing more from you and I'm really glad you got in touch.

Fondest Regards,

Peter x

PS: I've taken your advice and haven't included my telephone numbers or email addresses. Both of us could easily find them but it would spoil the magic of pen and ink, wouldn't it?

Chapter 11

The restaurant review isn't going well, not least because I'm distracted by Mr DJ's letter. I've read it so many times that I can recall most of it by heart. I'm amused by his style of putting things in question form – 'interrogatory style' as my old English teacher would have said – and his old fashioned use of words like 'chick' and 'playing the field'. Try as hard as I can, I can't remember what he sounded like back then. I know my friend Charlie always said that he sounded phony, 'trying to put on a corny Yankee accent' as she put it.

He has probably changed voice by now. I imagine a deeper, more cultured accent – sort of neutralised Home Counties with just a hint of his Midlands past. I've hung onto my Mid Country twang but have picked up a soft West Country lilt here and there. On the rare occasions I travel 'up country' – another Cornish expression – I'm often asked if I come from Bristol. As if.

'Be careful what you wish for' was one of David's favourite sayings, and I suppose it sums up my reaction to Mr DJ's letter. In theory I should be on cloud nine that he's welcomed my approach and has

even sent those photos of his family. He hasn't
included either of his former wives but I can see that
the children take after him, especially with those
distinctive hooded eyes and dark wavy hair.

It's the 1974 picture I'm staring at now and if I'm
honest, it's cringe worthy. This sex god of the
Midlands night clubs just looks well – naff. Those
ridiculous bell bottomed high waisted trousers and
that awful tight cheese cloth shirt. And that slimy
smile to the camera, a sort of 'look at me, aren't I
gorgeous?' It was only a year before we met, so this
frozen image is the one that mesmerized me and all
those other teenage girls. To put it mildly, it doesn't
make my heart sing.

Perhaps Kevin is right. Trying to reach back into
the past is probably a road to abject disappointment.
Like trying those retro sweets that are all over the
place these days. Last Christmas Amy bought me a
giant jar of 1960s sweets with lots of fondly
remembered childhood favourites like Black Jacks,
Fruit Salads and Love Hearts. Whether it's changed
adult taste buds or just over rosy memories of
sweets past, they just weren't the same. They're still
languishing in my kitchen now, more ornament
than confectionary treat. Amy tried a few and
described them as 'gross' and I had to pretend to
disagree with her, good mum that I am. She's right
though.

Yes, be careful what you wish for.

The photos aside, Mr DJ's letter has also left me

with mixed feelings. At least he has remembered me, which is something I suppose. It's just that the memories seem a bit superficial – 'the girl in the purple dress' – and nothing about those passionate few weeks when we locked out the rest of the world for a few blissful hours. It's good that he recognised me as a 'free spirit' but then follows it with the put down about Cornwall, seeing me as 'city' type. Truro is a city damn it, a beautiful Cathedral one which just happens to be surrounded by stunning countryside. Perhaps he really does need to make that visit one day.

The magazine review piece still beckons and I can recognise a distraction technique when I see it. But a reply to Mr DJ just has to come first. Once I've got that out of my system, I'll knock the restaurant feature on the head.

I like the idea of making a ritual out of letter writing. I've got the special note paper but Mr DJ went further with his antique fountain pen. Last time I used a bog standard biro but today I've dug out the ink pen and pencil set that my parents bought me when I got better than expected O level exam grades. They have a beautiful glossy brown tortoise shell finish and have hardly been touched since the time they were purchased. The silver suede case has survived remarkably unscathed despite some tiny mildew marks on the base. There are even a handful of ink cartridges which must be way past their sell by date. That's if ink even has such a thing.

Putting the cartridge in place is a bit fiddly and I inwardly curse as a large splatter of the navy blue innards lands on my shirt sleeve.

It takes a few minutes for the pen to 'fire up', like an old engine that has lain unused for decades. But once it gets going, the flow is beautiful and I love the way it prompts you to write more slowly. The movement across the page is sensual, the earthy smell of the ink contrasting with the floral scented tones of the writing paper.

As Peter quite rightly asked, how are we going to catch up after all this time? The journalist in me knows that it won't work by random musings, disconnected thoughts penned as and when. No, we'll need some themes, good subjects to focus on in each letter. Think of it as a series of features, each looking at aspects of our lives now and then.

'Hello again Peter,

I can't say how delighted I was to get your letter. After a month I began to think that you didn't want to reply and I'd steeled myself up for a disappointment. Then I got your lovely reply, delayed even more by our new postman putting it through the wrong door! Anyway, I'm pleased that you want us to keep writing and you'll see that I've copied you and used a proper ink pen this time. It's taken me a little time to get the hang of it and I've managed to ruin one of my favourite shirts in the process. Still it's a great excuse not to rush.

Thanks for the photos. Your kids look very like you and you shouldn't be so critical of your appearance. Stylish and 'dapper' came to mind when I first saw a picture of you in your local newspaper. As for the 1974 one – well let's just remember that it really was the decade that style forgot. Sorry but those awful trousers and shirt did nothing for you. Neither did the heavy makeup do much for me as you rightly point out. Thanks too for your compliment about my magazine photo and the articles. Photoshop works miracles (there I've said it!) but like you I've not resorted to cosmetic surgery. But never say 'never'. Yes, we must meet in Cornwall some time if only to show you that Truro really is a city. So I'm still an urban girl at heart but with a love of the countryside and sea on the doorstep. The best of both worlds.

Sorry to hear about your marriage break downs and I'm sure we'll come back to that in future letters. On that note, can I make a suggestion? Rather than just writing backwards and forwards in a random way, how about we come up with some themes for each letter? I could suggest the first one and then it will be over to you for the next. We can carry on that way for as long as we like and at least we'll have something to focus on in each letter.

Assuming you are OK with this – please tell me if you're not – I'll suggest our first theme. How about our proudest life achievements so far?

I'll begin with mine. The first is marrying David who was my soul mate and everything else besides. I try now to think of all the happy times we had together and cherish each memory. I will never get over the pain of losing him so suddenly but at least we had a great marriage and a beautiful daughter.

Talking of which – Amy. Another of the best things in my life. I'm proud of how well she has coped with David's death and is forging her own path in life. Above all I like the way she has turned out, kind, feisty, a good listener and not afraid to stand up for the things she believes in. David and I haven't done a bad job with Amy and there isn't a day when she doesn't bring joy to my life. OK, I'm lying about the last bit – she can be a pain in the arse sometimes, as can all teenagers – but she is fundamentally a good kid.

Then there's my job. Writing for a living is a privilege which I don't take for granted. Financially, I'm better off now than I've ever been but I can't imagine myself not writing and I suppose this is another offshoot. You are right to remember that I worked in fashion but I'll confess now that it was all made up. I'll explain more in another letter but let's say that I ended up doing a job that I love and there are too few people who can say that.

Living in one of the most beautiful parts of the country has to be up there with my best life achievements. Knowing that I'm just a few miles away from some amazing beaches and stunning countryside, makes for a healthier and happier life. I can honestly say that I wouldn't want to live anywhere else, although I've seen some lovely parts of the world.

I'm proud of my new found independence and ability to cope on my own. Yes I have a mum who lives with my sister in Wales – more about them in future letters – but I *did learn from an early age to stand on my own two feet. I was only 16 when I first left home and I had to grow up pretty quickly.*

Finally, I'm pretty pleased with the person I've turned out to be. Of course I'm not perfect – you'll find out that soon enough! – but at this stage of my life I'm happy with the real me. I hope that doesn't sound too arrogant because I promise you that I do know my own faults as well. Perhaps that could be a future letter theme?

So these are my proudest achievements and now over to you. I've also enclosed some more recent photos including a few of David and Amy. I wish I had more from the 1970s but people didn't take a lot of photos in those days. Not like the obsession with 'selfies' taken on cameras and mobile phones today. We really are turning into narcissists but at least there will be no shortage of images in the future.

That's me then and I'm really looking forward to hearing back from you. It struck me earlier that I can't remember how you sounded way back then but it really doesn't matter that much anyway. I've now got a deadline to meet so it's sign off time for the pen and out with the laptop.

All the best,

Debbie

My hand is aching from the effort of slow handwriting but I'll leave off posting this for now. I want to make sure that I haven't left anything out.

Or - more likely - given too much away.

Chapter 12

Amy is due home for the weekend, so I've been stocking up with her favourite foods. She announced out-of-the-blue that she was turning 'veggie' last summer and after my relentless nagging about her consumption of fried chicken takeaways, how could I object?

Now I'm secretly wishing that she'd go back to her old carnivorous ways. It's a pain having to shop for things that I don't normally have in and despite Amy's reassurance that she 'really doesn't mind' if I scoff meat in front of her – oh yeh, like hell she doesn't – I can't bring myself to do it. So its veggie weekend for me too and a Sunday roast which perversely has no chicken or beef. My granny must be spinning in her grave.

My mood today isn't helped by a call from Elaine, the editor of Cornwall Now. Apparently the owner of the restaurant I've reviewed in this month's issue is far from happy. 'Bloody fuming in fact' she says sucking in her breath. Here's me thinking that I'd been quite the diplomat given the third-rate meal he served up. I even praised the undercooked apple crumble dessert, damn it. But no, he's whingeing on about my lacklustre review and threatening to pull his advertisements.

'So what am I supposed to do?' I ask. 'He's bloody lucky that I didn't tell the whole truth.'

Elaine, being her usual tactful self, comes up with a solution – the promise of a free advert in the next issue and to include some of his signature recipes in the magazine's Christmas Special.

'God help anyone following his recipes for Christmas!' I snap before ending the conversation there and then. As soon as I put the phone down, I regret my tetchy response. It can't be easy being an editor and trying to juggle would-be advertisers with pesky writers. No doubt we'll laugh it off over a bottle of wine but I'm planning a full on sulk at least until the next magazine team meeting.

It's occurred to me that three weeks have passed since I posted off my last letter to Mr DJ. I've already checked with my neighbour, Ted, that he hasn't received any stray post.

'No – everything is always fine with our usual man Bob' Ted reassured me. 'It's only those drippy student types they use who get it wrong. Useless as a chocolate fire guard that lot.'

In the end I didn't make any changes to the last letter. Better to be spontaneous rather than over thinking things – after all, it's not a feature article but a chatty written exchange between two grown ups.

I jump when my phone bleeps that I have a text.

'Mum – my train is delayed so I won't be home until after 6. I'll text you again when we get nearer to Truro. Can't wait to catch up properly. Xxx'

Ah well – it gives me extra time to make sure Amy's room is just right. Last time she stayed over it was half finished with newly plastered walls. Now it is painted in her favourite shade of lilac, with a feature wall covered in a dramatic silver grey textured paper. There are some snazzy new pictures too and a large wall montage of family photos. I've bought her the double size bed she's always wanted because I guess that sooner or later she'll want to invite a boyfriend over. It's one of those awkward parent/child conversations I haven't had to face yet but I suspect it won't be too long coming.

Tonight's meal is Moroccan vegetables done in the Tagine a friend bought for me as a house warming present. I'd prefer to add some lamb but it smells pretty good anyway. I've got a yoghurt mint dip and some couscous to go with it. So it will be a relaxed evening at home and tomorrow I've booked some film tickets and a table at our favourite Italian restaurant. There is bound to be more good humoured banter between the owner, Umberto, and Amy over her conversion to vegetarianism. I can just hear him now.

'What? You are cutting out succulent meats? You must be out of your tiny mind! All those delicious morsels, the food of the gods…'

He thinks it's a stupid fad that she'll get over when she finally comes to her senses. She's got a bet with him that it 'ain't going to happen mate'. So we'll see.

I'm just putting the finishing touches to Amy's room when the doorbell screams out. I say 'screams' because someone is pressing it down hard and not letting go.

'Hang on – give me a minute.' I'm running down the stairs still clutching the new throw I was about to put on Amy's bed.

I can't quite make out the figure behind the door because it is raining hard and dark. Expecting it to be Ted, I'm taken aback to see Kevin who looks deadly pale and is visibly shaking.

'What the..? Are you OK? Come in out of that rain.'

He is staring back at me but looks completely out of it.

'Kevin – what the hell is up? Get in here now, you're frightening me.'

I grab hold of his hand and he flinches as if he's only just realised I'm there. Suddenly there are tears cascading down his face.

'Debbie she's gone. Left with the kids for Christ sake.'

Chapter 13

It takes me a good half hour to get any sense out of Kevin. When he does finally calm down – after a large mug of tea chased by a good tot of whisky – the story starts to unfold. And to put it mildly, I'm as shocked as he is.

'Debbie I swear I didn't see this coming. Not a bloody clue.'

I nod sympathetically but it isn't something I've experienced, thank God. Yes David and I had times when our relationship was strained, when we'd bicker and snap. Let's admit it, who doesn't in a long term partnership? But it never got to the boiling point of walking out.

With the whisky kicking in, Kevin's mood is shifting from shock to anger.

'The bitch. How could she? The poor kids will be confused, they like their routine….' He tails off mid rant to take another swig of his drink and I notice that the glass is now empty.

'Do you want another cup of tea?' I ask, hoping he'll opt for that over alcohol.

'I'll have a bit more of the stronger stuff if you don't mind' he replies reaching across for the whisky bottle. I sneak an opportunity to glance at my watch. 5.00pm so Amy will be back within the hour. Hell's bells.

After another half hour of me listening and Kevin alternating between sobbing spouse and mad as hell dad, we're interrupted by a text from Amy.

'Sorry I'm going to have to take this Kevin.' I dive into the hallway and dial Amy's number.

'Hi Mum – we're just getting into Truro station so we might get cut off. You all right to give me a lift? It's peeing down out there.'

'Listen Amy – something has cropped up. My friend Kevin is here. It's a long story and I'll fill you in later. Just jump into a cab and I'll pay when you get here.'

'You OK mum? You sound a bit tense.'

'I'm fine but Kevin isn't. Look I need to get back to him so I'll see you soon. Don't worry it's just a domestic between him and his wife. Nothing you need to worry about.'

I can hear the clipped announcement that the train is pulling into Truro station.

'Fine mum, see you soon….' The line goes dead on the approach to the station, so I head back to Kevin. He's staring into space with a refilled tumbler of whisky. Clearly he's not going anywhere tonight.

'That was Amy and she'll be here soon. Look, best if you stay here. I've got plenty of food cooked and I'll make up a spare bed.'

Kevin is on the verge of tears again and I put my arms around him. This makes him worse and he begins to sob loudly, burying his head on my shoulder. I take the opportunity to move the whisky bottle out of his reach.

'You go to the bathroom to freshen up. We don't want Amy seeing you in this state do we?' He looks up and nods, wiping his eyes with his sleeve.

'Thanks Debbie, you're the best mate ever. Look, I'll make myself scarce for a bit to give you and Amy a chance to catch up. I could do with a walk.'

'Good idea.' I reply. 'It'll clear your head and you'll feel better after you've had something to eat.' Kevin nods and heads towards the bathroom, grabbing his still wet jacket. Then I walk with him to the front door and thankfully the rain has lessened.

'Everything will be fine Kevin, you wait and see' I say giving him another reassuring hug.

He shrugs and disappears down the drive. Right then - time to get some coffee on and dig out the makeshift blow up bed. Kevin will have to spend the night in the room that passes as my office but it's better than having him go back to an empty house.

I'm still sweating from the effort of getting to

grips with the ludicrous temporary air bed when I hear Amy's taxi pull up outside. She's dragging her huge suitcase on wheels which means only one thing: there's a student load of washing, with enough spare capacity to squirrel away as much food as she can. All courtesy of good old mum of course. Still it's great to see her and at least she's appreciative of my efforts with her room.

'Mum it looks gorgeous. I love it. Let me throw a few things in the wardrobe and then you can tell me what's going on.' She gives me a big kiss and I leave her cooing over my 'brilliant taste in decoration' and selection of family photographs.

Well at least she's happy.

A pot of coffee later and I've finally got Amy up to steam.

'Wow it's all going on with this Kevin guy mum. And here's you telling me that he's happily married.' She smiles across at me and I know what she's thinking.

'Well it's nothing to do with me, as far as I knew they were the perfect family. Just goes to show how wrong you can be.'

Amy kicks off her shoes and stretches out her long legs across the sofa.

'If you say so mum but all those nights out at the pub with you? I mean there can't be many happily married guys who regularly go out with their attractive older female work colleagues.' She lets out a laugh as I playfully lob a cushion across at her.

'Hey, less of the *old* you. Attractive is fine though. Anyway, aren't you the one who is always telling me that men and women can just be friends?'

'They can mum but once you're married and have a family, well things change. It's just how it is.' She smiles across at me with the certainty of youth but I have to admit she does have a point.

The trill of the doorbell signals Kevin's return. He does seem calmer now and I leave him to chat with Amy while I go to sort out the food.

This is going to be one heck of a long night and when Amy yells out 'Mum shall I open a bottle of wine?' I respond with a resounding 'yes!'.

How does that old saying go? *'In Vino Veritas'*.

Chapter 14

To say the evening is turning into a long one is putting it mildly. Amy made herself scarce shortly after midnight but Kevin and I are still sitting up at 3.30am. We've both gone beyond tipsy and somehow the conversation turns to Mr DJ. It is a blessed relief to talk about something other than Kevin's spouse walking on him. You can only pick at a sore for so long.

'So are you going to show me his letter then?' Kevin's voice has started to slur a bit but then so has mine.

'No, I've told you it's private. But it was a good letter and I've suggested we come up with, er, some themes'. I laugh as I stumble over the word 'themes'.

'Let me think Debbie – how about him explaining how he lied through his teeth about his age to seduce a schoolgirl back in the day? That would be a great theme wouldn't it?' He has that mischievous glint in his eye which I recognise as a wind up tactic. I try not to rise to the bait.

'Now, now Kevin. You know that's not fair. I lied

to him too and did as much of the running as he did. It takes two to tango and I certainly wanted to dance.'

'Dance – so that's what you call it?' He laughs and raises his eyes to the ceiling in mock distaste. Well, I think it's mock but perhaps it isn't.

'You know what I mean Kevin, stop being such a prick. I was quite grown up at the time, far more mature than most fifteen year olds and I was actually only a few weeks away from sixteen anyway.'

'Oh so that makes it all right then? Come on, most 15 or 16 year olds think they're grown up. It goes with the territory. But that's no excuse for a grown man going with a school girl.' He examines his empty glass but there's no way I'm opening another bottle, so I ignore the hint.

'Anyway, has the randy old goat replied to your latest letter?'

'Not yet but I think he will. And he's quite the respectable gent these days, if you must know.' I let the 'randy old goat' comment go and despite having consumed his own body weight in wine, Kevin knows it's time to back off the sarcasm.

'So you're still not going to show me his letter? Go on, what's the harm in it?' Typical Kevin. Like a dog with a sodding bone.

'No and I haven't even said anything to Amy

about it either.' I say the last bit in a whisper even though I know she'll be dead to the world by now. A more sensible girl than her supposedly grown up mum.

Kevin still isn't giving up and he manages to get me to tell him about the first letter theme, the things I'm most proud about in my life. When I mention my marriage to David and Amy, the tears are starting to well up in his eyes. Shit, how could I be so tactless? This really is time for bed and I pack Kevin off with a giant mug of black coffee.

Predictably, Amy is first up all bright and bushy tailed. I feel half dead and my hair is sticking out like one of those Gonk toys I used to have as a kid. No sign of Kevin yet which I'm pleased about. I put my ear to his makeshift bedroom door and I can just about make out a continuous snoring sound. Best to leave him be and make myself human again.

'Mum you look terrible.' Amy is handing me a slice of toast which I grab hold of gratefully.

'Thanks Amy. Just what your mum wants to hear. But yes, I feel as bad as I look.' I take a large bite of the toast, wincing as the crust scratches the roof of my mouth.

'So what time did you two old lushes get to bed last night then?' Amy is clutching a teeming basket of washing and it's clear she's been up for hours. The hair and makeup are picture perfect and I can see her breakfast dishes soaking in the sink.

'Oh I don't know - three o'clockish? Can't remember. Any chance of a mug of tea to go with the toast?'

'Trade off. You put my washing on and I'll make you tea.' She hands me the basket and heads across to fill the kettle. I can feel my stomach lurch as I bend over to load the washing machine but just about manage to resist the urge to throw up.

'Here mum, get this down you.' Amy hands me the 'The World's Best Mum' mug she bought me last Mother's Day and I head off to the bedroom before there's a chance of Kevin getting to see me in this state. After a long shower topped up with more tea and toast, I'm beginning to emerge from my self induced stupor.

Kevin doesn't make it out of bed until midday and he looks even worse than I did.

He grunts when I sarcastically wish him 'Good morning.'

I leave him to make his way to the bathroom and Amy suggests that she makes him an egg sandwich 'which is great for hangovers'. Really? I always thought it was bacon sandwiches but I won't be so cruel as to inflict that task on my newly veggie daughter. Shame because I could murder a bacon sarnie myself.

I swear that Kevin's face changes colour when Amy suggests her hangover cure.

'Nah count me out Amy. The thought of food makes me retch. I'll stick to the water for now and any aspirin if you've got it.' He plonks himself down on the sofa, looking no better than when he first got up. I'm hoping he'll recover quickly enough to get going soon but it isn't looking that way.

As if reading my mind, Kevin glances across and manages a lop-sided grin.

'Don't worry Debbie I'll be out of your hair as soon as my stomach settles. You've been a great mate but I don't want to out stay my welcome.'

'Oh you don't have to rush off Kevin. Stay and see if you can manage a bite of lunch. I could rustle up some soup if you like.' Why am I such a people pleaser and liar to boot? I'm my own worst enemy.

'Forget the soup. You've done more than enough and I need to get back home to sort this bloody mess out.' He clutches the side of his head and quickly swallows the two aspirins that Amy hands him. I signal to Amy to disappear and sit down alongside Kevin.

'You sure you're OK to do that? I don't like the thought of you being there all weekend on your own. You could come back around here tomorrow for Sunday lunch if you want.'

Kevin manages a laugh but the effort makes him clutch at his head again.

'Jeez Debbie will you stop mentioning food? It's

like torture to a man with a frigging hangover from hell. And don't worry I'm not going to do anything stupid – I just need to think things though for a bit on my own. You enjoy the rest of the weekend with that lovely daughter of yours.'

A few hours later I'm watching Kevin reverse off the drive and notice a cream envelope protruding from my letter box.

I quickly stuff it in my pocket and can feel my heart racing. But I'm not going to read the contents until my daughter is on her way back to university. It's her turn for some attention now.

Even Mr DJ can wait.

Chapter 15

The house seems ridiculously quiet now that Amy has headed back to university, her suitcase a lot heavier than when she arrived. Feeling guilty about inflicting Kevin's domestic problems on her, I treated her to an impromptu shopping trip on Saturday afternoon. It was supposed to be a mission in search of new winter boots, after I'd noticed how tatty her existing pair looked. But inevitably we came home laden with bags and most of it was for Amy. Add to this the raid on my kitchen cupboards for everything from biscuits to tinned soup, and you have the picture. It took two of us to get the suitcase on the train and I swear I've put my left shoulder out. Still, I'm already missing her cheeky banter and most of all the laughter.

Time now to open that letter. I put the envelope to my nose and it's the same scent as before. Vanilla with a spicy after note. There's a feint whiff of cigar smoke, a smell I've become familiar with since moving in here. While still unable to rid the house of the previous owner's smoking habits, I'm starting to get there. This smell though is mellower and I guess that means more expensive tobacco.

It is quite a thick letter, several pages longer than the last one. The pen is different this time - at a guess a thinner nib - and the ink is a paler shade of blue.

Hello Debbie,

Yet again I have to start with an apology – I hope it doesn't become a habit. I've been on my travels again, this time to my villa in Los Gigantes, Tenerife. (I've enclosed a picture). It is partly to escape this awful British weather and partly to fulfil another little hobby of mine. Now it's confession time. When I'm over there, I do a 1970s night at a local hotel. (I can hear you snigger as you read this!). It's a chance to dig out the old music favourites and keep my hand in at DJ-ing. It's a hoot and the night gets packed out. Occasionally a punter gets hauled off to the hospital for over doing things on the dance floor – I kid you not – but most of the time it's a chance to catch up with fellow 1970s music enthusiasts. Before you ask, no I don't call myself 'Mr DJ' anymore – that would be too sad. Now I simply call the show ' 70s Disco Night'. Keeps things simple and says what it is, a fun trip down music memory lane

I loved the photos you sent of David and Amy. David looks ruggedly healthy and I was taken aback that it was only a few weeks before he died. So tragic that he lost his life at such a young age. Amy has certainly inherited some good genes from you and David. She's a real stunner and I'm sure will break some hearts.

I like your idea for themes for our letters. From what I remember, you always were one for organising things even at a young age. I seem to recall that the only time my flat got sorted out was when you were around and you'll be pleased to know that I'm a much tidier person these days. When you've shelled out for a home and furniture, you want to show it off don't you?

So now you've got me thinking about my life's proudest achievements. Where to start, work or personal? I'll kick off with the personal stuff and here it has to be my three great kids. Lulu is all grown up now and works for a record company in London, a real chip off the old block. She's got a steady boyfriend and there's talk of them getting married. I also know she's getting broody, so I hope I'll be a grandad soon. I quite like the idea of that actually. (I never thought I'd relish the prospect of being a grandad but most of my friends are already there and loving it). When I drop my younger boys off to school, people think I'm their grand-daddy which is hardly surprising.

Freddie and Gene are a joy and I've been around a lot more for them than I was for Lulu. I share access (hate that word) with their mum and in the school holidays, they spend time with me in Tenerife. They are twins but have different personalities, likes and dislikes. I'm enjoying that nice stage between early childhood and teenage angst – it won't be long before they start to chose their friends over being with the old man.

Unlike you, I'm not proud of my marriages and both were terrible mistakes. Apart from the kids that is. So I'll gloss over this part of my life if you don't mind. Perhaps later on I'll go into the reasons why my marriages failed but not now when I'm supposed to be looking at my *proudest life achievements!*

Sticking to the personal, I'm proud that I've got the house that I want and the resources to live my life as I chose. There aren't many people who enjoy that luxury, don't you agree? I've got some long standing good friends and have proved to be a loyal mate to them. I hope that when I die I'll be remembered as a generally nice bloke. (If that doesn't sound too big headed).

Next – let me think. Physical fitness, Yes, I'm certainly proud of that achievement given the excesses of the 70s. I still like a drink but the hard boozing and the dope went out of the door years ago. Now I have a home gym and I walk for miles. It gives me the energy for those Tenerife discos and the nights in with my women friends. It's true that a 70s leopard doesn't change his spots!

Now for the work achievements. I know you've been doing your homework here, so I don't need to go into masses of detail. I suppose my proudest moment was getting the 'Music Publicist Of The Year' award. It was a great note to retire on and I was delighted to get the recognition from my peers in the music publishing industry. Out with a bang as they say?

What else work-wise? I suppose my vintage record collection and music memorabilia. I've no idea what it is really worth these days but I'm guessing quite a bit. Come to think of it, I'm actually quite proud of my early DJ days. I played some ground breaking music back then and helped to get a number of Northern clubs up and running. I've lost count of the number of bands I helped out in those early days and it allowed me to get established in the London music publicity scene.

I'm starting to run out of these proudest achievements now, so I'll suggest the next theme. How about 'happiness' and what has been the best time of your life so far?

I hope everything is going well with your new place and that Amy is enjoying her course. I see that you're still writing for Cornwall Now and I've decided to take out a subscription. After all, I didn't even realise that Truro was a city as you rightly pointed out – I've always thought of it as a county town.

You mentioned that you couldn't remember what I sounded like back in the day. Well, I was a broad Brummie then but now my accent has softened a lot more. I still drop the odd Brum word in here and there but my accent is more neutral these days. I hope that at some point in the future you'll get to hear it for real. You'll see from the handwriting that I'm starting to get writer's ache now – I'm trying out a different pen but I think I'll go back to my other one next time.

I'm looking forward to hearing your news and your thoughts on my 'happiness' theme. Promise to get back quicker next time as I'll be staying put for a few months.

Bye for now,

Peter xx

PS: Send some more photos. I'd love to see your new house......

Chapter 16

I'm staring hard at the picture Mr DJ has enclosed of his villa in Tenerife. It is a massive pale lemon building in the classic Mediterranean style – windows with white shuttered blinds to shield the rooms from the fierce afternoon sun and lots of pretty Bougainvillea plants growing around the walls. I can see the swimming pool in the distance and the grounds are neatly manicured but not overly so. It has a welcoming feel despite the imposing size and I can only imagine how great it must be to own this as a second home. He has certainly done well for himself.

This latest letter is more relaxed, chatty even. It's interesting how he has separated his proudest achievements between the personal and work related ones. It shows a disciplined, methodical way of thinking that I would never have associated with the old 'Mr DJ' Peter. It just goes to show how much he has changed and that we still have a lot to learn about each other.

I also like the fact he's proud of his children and is looking forward to being a grand-daddy. He's right that I find his 1970s night amusing but in a smiley way rather than the 'sniggering' he suggested. I remember when David and me went on a holiday to Cyprus and every night we'd hear '60s and '70s music blasting out from a nearby hotel. We'd joke about the types of people who would want to relive their youth on a holiday disco floor and one night we popped our heads in when curiosity got the better of us.

I remember the club was awash with 'grey mops' as we dubbed them, probably no older than I am now. One old boy in a loud Hawaiian shirt was strutting his stuff to an old Kinks record, throwing his arms in the air like it was 1966 all over again. I wanted to stay put, as it was good fun people watching, but David dragged me away saying that the place was depressing, full of old 'coffin dodgers'. Strange to think that David only had about 20 years to live when we took that holiday. He would never make it to be a 'grey mop'.

Here I am decades later, reading that an ex-boyfriend is putting on a similar show in Tenerife. I wonder if other young couples are laughing at the spectacle, just as we did? Perhaps one day I'll get to see one of his shows - you never know.

His choice for our next letter theme is intriguing and I'll need to give it some thought. Happiest time of my life so far? There are so many good memories that I'm going to be spoiled for choice. Hmm. Not the easiest of themes and I don't want to rush into this one. If he is staying put for a few months, then there is no need to wing off a reply straight away.

Anyway, time to stop mulling over this latest letter and get back to the piece I'm trying to write about a local artist who is making a name for himself in 'driftwood art.' Basically, he collects old bits of driftwood from local beaches and turns it into wall art. It's become quite popular in these parts and a couple of the national style magazines have picked up on the trend. 'Beach Chic' as one publication has called it. I quite like this guy's work and I'm thinking of buying one of his pieces for my hallway. Driftwood in a bathroom would be too naff for words.

The tape recorded interview with him is a bit hit and miss on sound quality. He kept moving across the room to show me some of his latest pieces while babbling away at the same time. It has reminded me to get a new recorder, one of those fancy digital ones rather than my ten year old 'relic' as Amy calls it.

Perhaps I can drop a hint to her for my Christmas present? Although knowing Amy, I'll end up with an all singing and dancing one that I'll have to take a course to fathom out. When I bought my latest mobile phone, the sales assistant suggested that I attend a 'familiarisation' day at their store. What? To use a phone? I still don't use half the features or 'apps' and call me old fashioned, but what is wrong with a phone being just a thing that you call people up on?

Almost on cue, I pick up my mobile to do just

that – talk. Kevin has called me to supposedly check when I'll be able to deliver my feature and how many photographs I'm likely to use. In reality, he's keen to chat about the latest development with his estranged wife Gilly.

'So how are things on the home front?' I ask, rising to the bait.

Kevin sighs and drops his voice.

'Not much different. She's still living at her mum's place with the kids but at least they are going to school and are taking it well considering. I think they see it as a sort of adventure with their nan. We've told them that we are just spending a little time apart for now because daddy has a big project on at work. I think the oldest has twigged there is something more to it though.'

'Well at least they're in a place they know and only a few miles away. It's not like they are staying at some awful rented place and kids are quite adaptable. What about Gilly, have you managed to talk properly yet?'

Another sigh from Kevin and I can imagine him raking his hands through his hair, like he usually does when stressed.

'She's suggesting counselling but I'd rather we sat down face to face to talk first without involving a sodding stranger. I've suggested we meet up this week and she says she'll think about it. Hang on a minute Debbie.' I can hear someone in the background and a few minutes go by while he discusses page layouts.

'Sorry about that Debbie but you know what it's like near deadline day. Listen, how about you and me going out for a pizza or something tonight if you're not doing anything? My treat and it would be great to catch up.'

I'd planned a pampering night in with a long soak, face pack and the rest of my box set of escapist American drama. But I can hear the desperation in Kevin's voice and understand his reluctance to go back to his now empty house.

'You're on Kevin but let's not make it a boozy one. I've still got my feature to do and I don't want to write it with a headache.'

'Agreed Madam. So shall I see you about 7.30pm at Bits and Pizza? I'll book a table to make sure we get a nice quiet corner'. I can make out the sound of someone else coming into Kevin's office so we end the conversation abruptly.

The driftwood feature will have to wait for now, as I'm off for that bath and pamper anyway. My unexpected dinner date will be a good excuse to try out those new skin tight jeans Amy persuaded me to buy on our shopping trip.

After all, the legs still have it.

Chapter 17

'Bits and Pizza' is a favourite haunt of Cornwall Now staff, tucked away from the main shopping street in Truro. The name is naff but the food is always first rate, especially the wood fired pizzas. Not a slate plate or rustic reference in sight, just good unpretentious cooking and value for money as well. No wonder it's packed out on a dull late Monday evening.

We decide to have some dough balls to start with and then share a large seafood pizza with a side salad. As we promised ourselves, there is no wine tonight - just fruit juice and water.

I can't help noticing how much weight Kevin has lost. Not that he was a big man to begin with but now his blue linen shirt looks several sizes too big. He has dark rings under his eyes and looks like he has aged 10 years in the week that has passed since Gilly walked out with the kids.

'You look like you're disappearing' I joke as we wait for our food to arrive.

'Not had much appetite to be honest. I've been living on sandwiches with the odd trip to the local fish and chip shop. Usually I end up throwing most of it away. A good diet tip eh? The buy and chuck away weight loss plan – do you think it could take off?' It's good to see that he still has a sense of humour and I reassuringly squeeze his hand across the table.

'Nah people want that miracle diet where they can eat what they want and still lose weight. Now that would be a best seller. Nothing like stress though to make the pounds fall off as I know only too well.'

We laugh as our waiter comes over with a mound of garlic butter dough balls and I push them towards Kevin.

'Right then Kevin, get tucked in. We need to bulk you out.' He nods and picks up a dough ball, popping it into his mouth in one go.

We spend the next few minutes in silence as we dig into our starter and I'm pleased to see that for tonight at least, Kevin has got some of his old appetite back.

Our waiter comes over to ask if everything is OK and we both give the thumbs up.

'Can I get you anything else to drink?' the waiter asks as he eyes our near empty glasses. I know Kevin would love a beer but a pledge is a pledge, so we order more orange juice.

While we wait for the main course, I lighten the

conversation by asking if he's picked up on any gossip from the magazine. Now that I'm doing fewer features, there is no real need for me to go into the office. So I'm even more cut off from things than before and only manage to catch up with the rest of the editorial team when we have the occasional big brainstorm meeting.

Kevin leans across the table in a conspiratorial way.

'Rumour has it that there's going to be a new boss to shake things up a bit. A sort of super manager who is being brought in by the publisher. Elaine won't like that one little bit.'

I'm still feeling miffed by Elaine's attitude to the complaint about my restaurant review but at least you know where you are with her, warts and all. This new guy – and I somehow think it will be a man – sounds a bit sinister.

'So I suppose that will mean more upheaval, more uncertainty. I doubt whether this new bod will leave things untouched, people like that never do.' As the words tumble out of my mouth, I can see that I'm adding to Kevin's woes, on top of everything else. Time then, for a quick change in subject.

'Hey meant to tell you. I got another reply from Peter the other day. His suggestion for our next letter theme is happiness, defining it and describing the happiest day of my life so far.' I laugh, a little too loudly, as I top up my water glass.

Kevin cocks his head to one side, his expression changing quickly from concern over possible turmoil at his workplace to something approximating amusement.

"Ha that's a good one. I bet it's got you thinking. Sounds like you two are planning a course in philosophy in your dotage.' Kevin's eyes are twinkling at the prospect of winding me up.

'Hey, less of the 'dotage' you. He might be old but I'm still a spring chicken by comparison.' At this point I'm wishing I hadn't worn those tight jeans picked out by Amy. After downing two large slices of pizza, I feel like my stomach is about to explode out of a modern equivalent of a corset.

'Yeh you're aging well Debbie. Isn't there a name for glamorous middle-aged women? Cougars....?'

I kick him under the table and he feigns a look of pain. The couple on the next table glance across and I'm sure they think we are just another couple clowning around on a night off from domestic responsibilities. Or should that be a Cougar enjoying her date night?

Out of the corner of my eye, I spot Elaine coming through the restaurant front door. She's obviously been working late and has called by to collect a takeaway. She looks preoccupied and a few minutes go by before she sees Kevin and me.

I take the opportunity to warn Kevin who hasn't noticed anything.

'Psst Elaine's just walked in. She'll be over here in a minute.'

I wave across as she makes her way towards us, trying to navigate between the packed tables.

'Hi you two. Mind if I join you while I wait for my pizza?' She looks at both of us, trying to work out if she's interrupting an important dinner date or just two friends catching up.

'No problem – pull up a chair' I reply breezily while Kevin just looks plain awkward. I'm not sure whether he's told Elaine about his marital problems but I suspect that he hasn't.

Elaine leans across to the table behind us, asking the two diners whether it is all right for her to have a spare chair. They nod in unison, mouths full of whatever they are eating.

Throwing her coat across the back of her seat, she positions herself in front of us. Suddenly it feels a bit like an editorial meeting and I expect her to whip out her laptop.

'So Debbie, how are things with you?'

I'm just about to answer when Kevin interrupts, asking Elaine if she'd like a drink while she waits.

'Go on then, I'll have half a lager. I see you two are being good tonight and staying off the booze.'

I smile and shrug as Kevin beckons over the waiter.

'I've been drinking a bit too much recently, so I told Kevin I'd share a pizza with him as long as we stayed off the alcohol.' Kevin pulls a mock 'hard done by' face, looking covetously as Elaine's lager arrives.

It's not long before the subject strays on to the new manager who is due to start with Cornwall Now in a few weeks time.

'Kevin's told you about this new bloke?' Elaine asks between a sip of her lager.

'Ah, so it is a *he* then? We were just talking about it when you walked in' I respond, scanning her face for a reaction. But she's giving nothing away.

'Well, I suppose it's an opportunity to get another experienced eye on the magazine. You can get too close to things when you've been editing it for as long as I have.' She takes another sip of her drink and a slight red flush on her neck is the only sign that she's under pressure.

'As long as it's not just change for changes sake' Kevin chips in, clearly linking this development to that other big upheaval in his life.

Change for changes sake. The words hover in the air for a few moments.

'You're right Kevin but it's up to me – I mean the team – to fight our corner. We know Cornwall and our readers. I think it will take a little while for this Carl Martin guy to find his feet. This isn't trendy

North London after all.' Elaine coughs as she realises that she has just let slip the new manager's name.

'Listen you two; I don't want his name getting out before we go properly public on this with the rest of the staff. Can I trust you both? We'll be making an announcement later this week.'

We nod to reassure her that the information is safe with us.

'Great, thanks for that. Anyway here's my food, so I'll leave you two to get on with the rest of your evening. Debbie, we should to get together soon to discuss your next few features. Give me a call tomorrow and we'll put something in the diary.'

And with that she is off, leaving Kevin and me beaming that we are the first to know the name of the new magazine big wig.

Carl Martin.

So, what's the betting that we'll both be hitting the internet search engines when we get home tonight?

Chapter 18

It is supposed to be an early evening meal and straight back to my DVD box set. The best laid plans and all that.

After finishing our meal Kevin insists on driving me back home, ignoring my pleas that 'it's only a 10 minute walk.' Of course that leads to me inviting him in for a coffee – yes, that old cliché. But hand on heart it's exactly what I mean.

I fancy some proper coffee, so while I'm sorting out the machine and filter papers Kevin gets straight onto my computer to search out Carl Martin.

Within minutes he's back in the kitchen, clutching a print out.

'Hey, guess what Debbie? This Carl Martin guy is quite a big fish in publications. He's worked on a stack of national glossies in London including some big newspaper magazines. It must have taken some persuasion to get him on board for Cornwall Now. Here, take a look.'

He hands me the print out and I quickly scan the details. Mid-forties, privately educated followed by Politics, Economics and Philosophy at Oxford and then straight into a leading style magazine. The accompanying picture shows him to be urbane, with a greying but full head of hair and stylishly dressed in a dark blue suit with what looks like the palest of grey cashmere sweaters underneath. Smart but not overly so. He has steely greyish green eyes and an angular face with full prominent lips. The overall look is confident, self possessed and he's clearly someone who hasn't had to fight hard for his success.

'Well no wonder Elaine is worried' I comment, handing the paper back to Kevin.

'Looks like a right smug bastard' he replies, taking another look at the picture.

'Now Kevin, don't be so quick to judge. He might turn out to be just the thing the magazine needs. Still, it's a bit of a curve ball move onto a magazine in Cornwall.' I pass Kevin the coffee pot and we head into the living room.

Now it's 2.00am and here I am, lying in bed with Kevin fast asleep beside me. One minute we were lounging on the sofa, sipping coffee and putting the world to rights. Next thing we're kissing passionately, clothes discarded on the floor and I'm leading Kevin into the bedroom. You can guess the rest and the sex was pretty damn good too.

Shit, what the hell have I done? None of this was planned and Kevin still has a wife and two kids. Just because she's walked out doesn't mean…..

I slip out of the bed and thankfully Kevin doesn't wake up. Tip toeing my way downstairs, I clear away our clothes strewn across the sofa and the floor. There's no way I can sleep now, so I log on to my computer and make a half-hearted stab at my feature on the driftwood artist. But I can't concentrate and instead I make my way to Amy's room and clamber into her bed. At some point I must have nodded off because I'm awoken by a loud knock on the door.

'Debbie you in there? ' Before I have a chance to respond, Kevin's head appears from behind the door and there's a few moments of sheepish silence, with neither of us knowing what to say.

Shit, shit, shit.

It's me who breaks the silence.

'Bloody hell Kevin what were we thinking about? You have a wife and we're best mates damn it.'

'With benefits now' he replies sitting down on the edge of the bed. He smiles but I don't feel able to return it. This is much too complicated for humour.

'Come on Debbie, we're two grown ups and we had sex. Big deal. It's hardly the crime of the century and I for one don't regret a thing.' He reaches across but I flinch and pull the duvet up towards my chin.

'Look Kevin, last night was something that just happened and I don't know why. But that's where it should stay, a one off. You're still with Gilly.'

'Just about. She was the one who went off, not me remember? If you want last night to be a one night stand then fine but I hope you don't start beating yourself up about it. We had some fun didn't we?'

Fun. Yes we certainly did. But things don't look quite so devil-may-care in the cold light of day.

'I'll make some breakfast' I say, deciding that avoidance is the best tactic for now.

'Fine but don't go to any effort for me. Coffee will do. You sure you're OK Debbie?' He touches my arm and I respond with a forced smile. OK? Like hell I am and I'm inwardly cursing myself for being such a stupid cow.

To say that the next half hour is awkward is putting it mildly. I try keeping out of Kevin's way, taking my time having a shower and logging onto the computer while he gets ready for work. Suddenly my house feels too small.

After a perfunctory goodbye kiss and a promise to 'catch up later' I'm at last left on my own. The driftwood art feature distracts me for a few hours and then I decide to do a bit more digging on Carl Martin. From what I can gather he's single apparently, although he's been linked to a good number of women. Most of these are of a certain type – glossy models or wealthy socialites. He seems to go for rake thin olive skinned brunettes from the pictures I've seen so far. I wonder whether he's met someone in Cornwall? If not, he'll certainly be seen as a real catch and there is no shortage of his preferred type down here.

I'm distracted from my research by a call from Elaine.

'Hi Debbie. You able to talk now?'

'Fine Elaine. You've got me at a good time - I've just finished the driftwood feature. How's your day going?'

'Mad as usual, nothing new there. I've just bumped into Kevin and asked him again to keep quiet about the thing I mentioned last night. You won't talk about it to anyone, will you Debbie?'

'Of course not, you know I won't. But I have done a little bit of digging and this Carl Martin is an interesting guy.' I wait for her response which is a few seconds coming.

'Yeah, well let's see. He's due to start the week after next and will be shadowing me for the first few days. That's partly what I'm calling you about. There will be a full editorial meeting a week on Friday. Can you make that?'

'Yes that's fine' I reply circling the date on my desk calendar.

Elaine gives a small cough and I can hear her tapping something into the computer in her office.

'I'd like plenty of ideas for future issues, just to show him what a talented team I have. You're our best ideas person Debbie so I'll be relying on you to come up with some gems.'

Good old Elaine with her 'flattery will get you everywhere'. Works every time.

'Of course – I'll get my thinking cap on. How did Kevin seem today by the way?'

Elaine seems momentarily stumped by my question.

'Same as usual, just like yesterday in fact. Why are you asking?'

Kevin let slip last night that he had already confided in Elaine about his problems with Gilly, so I know I'm on safe ground.

'Oh, it's just this business with his wife and kids. We had a bit of a heart to heart last night about it all. It hasn't been easy for him with that going on.' I know why I'm *really* asking about him and it's nothing to do with the marriage woes.

'Well Debbie these things happen and you know Kevin, he'll sort something out. I think he's taking everything quite well considering. I offered him some time off but he won't hear of it. '

We end the conversation with a promise of a girls' only night out at the end of the week. Elaine can be quite a laugh when she lets her editor guard down which isn't that often. But when she does –

boy, she does it with a vengeance.

I'm tempted to ring Kevin but resist the urge. Somehow though, the time seems right to start my next letter to Mr DJ. So out with the scented notepaper and the decades old fountain pen. Filling the pen with ink feels like a ritual, and I draw in the dark blue liquid slowly and deliberately. Then my hand moves across the page.

'Hi Peter…..'

Chapter 19

'I love the photos of your house in Tenerife – it looks fantastic and really imposing. It must be great just to be able to jet off into the sun whenever you please. Lucky you.

I did smile (not snigger!) when you mentioned your DJ sessions at a local hotel. Only because it reminded me of holidays in Cyprus with David. They had a similar retro night there but when you are younger, you just laugh at all the oldies reliving the past. Now it sounds like a good bit of fun which I'm sure it is. So keep on rocking!

I've been thinking about your chosen theme of 'happiness'. It seems an easy one until you have to single out those happiest moments. I've got so many to choose from but think I've narrowed it down now. So here goes...

My wedding day was one of the happiest days of my life. It wasn't a fancy wedding, just a local registry office, with a few close friends as witnesses. Dad was too ill to travel down (mum had to look after him) and my sister Carol was living in Germany at the time. But for us it was perfect, simple and unpretentious, though we splashed out on a posh country hotel for a few days away afterwards. It was an idyllic time of my life and I only wish it could have lasted longer.

The day Amy was born was another one of those memorable days, the ones you want to bottle forever. It was the middle of winter, bitterly cold, stormy and it was a difficult birth to put in mildly. Afterwards, all that paled into insignificance. She was the most beautiful thing I had ever seen

I have to stop writing because the tears are stinging my eyes. But it's not the memories of getting married or giving birth to Amy that has caused this. There is something else gnawing away in the background, an ache that has recently resurfaced in my life although it has never really gone away. 'Come on Debbie, get a grip girl', I mutter under my breath. Now isn't the time to dwell on it, especially as I'm trying to focus on my happiest times and memories. Call it telepathy or sheer coincidence, but a text from Amy arrives with impeccable timing.

'Afternoon mum - just off to a lecture now but are you up for a Skype chat this evening – assuming you're not out with that Kevin mate of yours? Let me know the best time to call. BTW I'm really getting into the cooking now and made a shepherd's pie last night which was awesome or so I'm told! Catch up later. Xx'

I wince at the reference to Kevin and reply that tonight at 8.00pm is fine. Usually our chats last for an hour or so, which will be a welcome distraction.

Back to my letter then.

'...*a precious new life and a very special daughter. I know everyone thinks their children are brilliant but my Amy really did turn out to be exactly that, especially the way that she coped with her dad's death at an early age.*

Moving down to Cornwall all those years ago. It is so beautiful here that I can't imagine living anywhere else. Granted, the English weather stinks a lot of the time but we've got some incredible scenery and coastlines to die for. Waking up here every day makes me feel happy, even when it's raining.

Close friends also make me happy and I have one really special one who happens to be a guy. His name is Kevin.....'

I pause again mid sentence and can't help thinking how this bit would have been easier to write if it hadn't been for last night. Before then it had been a mildly flirtatious but platonic relationship. Now though....well, I can't stray into that with Mr DJ. So let's just pretend it didn't happen.

'*His name is Kevin and we work together on the magazine. He's married with two kids and is a decade younger than me. We just seem to click and he is my best friend and confidante. He was so supportive when David died, is a great soul mate and above all makes me laugh.*

Work too is a source of joy and I love the variety of stuff I get to write about. Everything from restaurants to people who make art out of bits of wood washed up on the beach – in case you're wondering, I've just finished a feature on a driftwood artist by the way. So you'll get to read it in the next issue. You clearly love your work too, so we've both been lucky to find something that has been fulfilling. You've definitely made more money though!

I was dreading moving house but now that I have, it's a great little home. The décor and furniture are all to my taste and the fresh start has been a welcome distraction. My new little nest is still a work in progress but I love tracking down a new piece of furniture or a new piece of art.

Other things that make me happy – scented baths, new shoes, fresh flowers and of course, chocolate. (Such a girly I can hear you saying - but true).

I'm going to embarrass you now but I still have happy memories of our afternoons in that pokey little bedsit of yours. The summer seemed endless and the fact we had to meet in secret just made it all the more special. Of course I was devastated .....

Another pause. Now I'm straying onto dangerous territory but hell, what's the point of these letters if we don't tell the truth?

Truth. A simple word that is anything but. What we're really talking here is a version of the truth.

'....when you left for Manchester. But it was the summer that I started to grow up and your move gave me the push to move to another part of the country.'

I jump as my phone rings out.

'Hi it's Kevin. You all right to talk?'

My carefully constructed letter, delicately and precisely written, now has a great inky smudge at the end of the last sentence.

Not for the first time today, I mutter a small word under my breath.

Shit.

Chapter 20

My voice reflects irritation at being interrupted mid letter about the big subject of personal happiness.

'Oh hi Kevin.....'

He immediately picks up on my prickly tone.

'Look I can ring back later if you like. I just wanted to check how you are sweetheart.'

Sweetheart. Now where the hell did that little nugget come from?

'I'm fine Kevin, just in the middle of writing something. How are things with you?'

He pauses for a moment, as if he's weighing something up.

'Fine - I think - as long as what happened last night doesn't get in the way of our friendship. You know I'd really hate to lose you as a mate Debbie.'

Poor Kevin. He's right though. I'm being an over dramatic bitch about something that happened at a vulnerable time in his life. We should be able to move on and go back to where we were.

Should. Could. Would.

'Don't be silly Kevin. Of course it's not going to get in the way of our friendship. What's done is done and I think we should just try to forget about it. But I still think it's best if we leave off seeing each other for a few days. You need to concentrate on Gilly and the boys.'

Kevin sighs more in frustration than relief.

'Well as long as you mean that. You're a great friend and that's way more important than mere sex....'

His voice trails off, as if he is unsure what to say next. It's an excruciating call and I just want it to end.

'Listen Kevin, you're not getting rid of me that easily, so don't worry on that score. Look Amy is just about to call, so shall we just leave it at that? Still mates but we'll put a bit of clear blue water between ourselves until next week?'

'OK Debbie but let's not leave it too long to meet up. How about Sunday – if the weather's good, a long walk, followed by a pub lunch?'

'Fine, it's a deal. Isn't it tomorrow that you have your chat with Gilly?'

Another sigh, this time one more of resignation.

'Yeah and I'm not looking forward to that. We haven't really spoken much since she left and when we have it's all been about the boys. So a face to face is going to be hard.'

I wish him good luck and pretend that Amy is trying to get through on Skype. Thankfully he takes the hint and I'm left to get on with my letter.

'Apologies for the inky splodge just now. The phone rang out and I was so engrossed in my letter that it made me jump. Anyway, I think I've got to the end of my happiness musings and I look forward to hearing yours. I've been thinking about the next theme and the subject of 'regret' comes to mind. Do you have any big regrets and are you planning to put them right? I know I have some and I'd be surprised if you didn't, although I suspect you don't dwell too much on them. (So I'm going to make you!). I've enclosed a few photos of my 'new' house which is actually quite old as you'll see. The garden needs some serious work, so it will keep me busy over the coming months. I'm quite inspired by your Tenerife garden plants and I'm sure some of them would grow well in Cornwall. So over and out for now and I think your combination of happiest moments with biggest regrets should make a fascinating read.

Debbie x

It's the first time I've signed off with a cheeky 'x' mark but somehow it seems appropriate after this letter. We're getting less formal, more chatty and open. The art of writing a letter actually seems to increase intimacy in the way that a business like e-mail just can't do.

I take my time folding the paper and placing it

into the envelope. Carefully sealing the top down, I notice a small slick of mauve lipstick just above the address. Damn. First an inky splodge on the letter and now this.

But I'm not going to re-write the envelope. That lipstick is part of me and you know what? The brand may have varied over the years but I've always stuck to that same mauve colour.

So Mr DJ, some things don't change from the past.

You could also say that I've sealed things literally with a kiss.

Chapter 21

Not seeing Kevin for a few days has been tougher than I thought. I've got used to having him around, a mate to call on when I fancy a trip to the cinema or pub. This mini break has shown just how dependent I've become and how few other close friends I have. It's a lesson learned and I've resolved to do something about it.

When I speak to Amy, she keeps asking me if I'm all right.

'What's up mum? You sound, I don't know, a bit funny....'

I manage to laugh it off, putting it down to my age and just being a bit tired. I can tell she isn't convinced but there is no way I'm going to confide in her about what happened with Kevin. Yet another little secret I'm keeping from her.

Actually that 'little secret' pales into significance compared to the bigger one, the humdinger that I've not told anyone about and I mean *anyone*. I didn't even tell my husband David which - to put it mildly - was difficult. But there you have it, a classic case of secrets and lies.

Without Kevin's banter to distract me, I've been dwelling on the phone call I made a few months ago. It followed a letter I received from an adoption agency and as soon as I saw the brown official looking envelope I just knew.

It was him. 'Edward' as I named him back then, after the grandad I never met. The one my granny used to tell me about all the time over those cooking sessions in her little kitchen.

Edward would be 37 now. Imagine that. Much the same age as a lot of the people working on the magazine. He might even be a dad himself.

And now he wants to get in touch. He wants to meet his real birth mother, the one who handed him over to the adoption agency in the Spring of 1976. The agency note is brief and to the point but the message is clear. Do I want to make contact with my son? 'My son.' 'Contact.' The words are dancing in my head, sometimes slowly and other times crashing to a crazy tempo

Deep down I knew it would happen. Over the years I'd find myself thinking about him, especially on March 18, his birthday. What was he doing? Where was he living and was he happy?

Once – and only once – when Amy was a baby, I nearly told David. Unlike Edward's birth, Amy's had been a difficult one and I had to have an emergency caesarean, losing a lot of blood. I decided then and there that I didn't want another pregnancy and later on persuaded David to have 'the snip' as it's so cheerily called.

'But what if we change our minds, decide that we'd like another baby, a brother or sister for Amy? Shouldn't we just wait for a bit?'

I nearly blurted it out then. 'I do have another child, a boy...' Almost but didn't. Within a year the deed was done and David had the operation. So Amy was our only child and Edward receded again into the background, creeping into my thoughts just occasionally.

The woman on the end of the phone has a soft Liverpool accent and an understanding manner. A good listener and sympathetic. I don't know her from Adam but somehow it seems right to be discussing this massive dilemma I'm now facing.

'Take your time and have a good think before you decide what to do Debbie. There is no rush and I'm here if you need to talk it through more.' I could listen to her lovely sing song accent all day and we leave it that I will call her back once I have mulled things over.

'Mulled.' The word hardly does it justice.

I want to talk it through with my mate Kevin, like I do with most big decisions. But that would mean telling him something that even my own flesh and blood know nothing about, damn it.

My biggest worry is Amy. I've no idea how she

will take the news that she has a brother living in Canada who is hoping to come over to meet his long lost birth mother. He's not even called Edward anymore. His adoptive parents renamed him Andrew but kept Edward as his second name. From what I pick up from 'Liverpool Lil', my nickname for the adoption agency worker, Andrew and his new parents moved to Canada in the late 1970s. His adopted dad worked as a police officer and mum was a nurse. Andrew has thrived there, studied medicine and is now working somewhere in Toronto.

His adopted parents are still alive and are happy with his decision to try to make contact with me.

Lil has a phone contact number for Andrew which she says she'll let me have once I've decided what I'd like to do. Meantime, how would I feel if Andrew wrote me a letter, telling me more about himself and his reasons for wanting to get in touch? Again there's no hurry to make a decision she said. That is her soothing mantra – 'no hurry.'

So I'm biding my time and if I'm honest, this has been the biggest reason for contacting my first time lover, Mr DJ.

Now I have another new correspondence to consider, with the threads of the past twisting and turning into an uncertain cloth.

It might seem odd but I'd prefer to see a photo of my son first before I read anything else about him.

Just a photo, a face.

Then I'll know for sure what I need to do next.

Chapter 22

I can't help noticing how spruced up everyone is for our first meeting with new magazine boss Carl Martin. It's as if everyone has put on their Sunday best clothes and even the office has been given a good tidy. Kevin is wearing a smart suit and tie rather than his usual uniform of casual jumper and jeans. He smiles across as I take my seat next to Elaine who has also made an effort with a pale blue dress. As for me, I've opted for a tailored white blouse and smart black trousers. Come to think of it, we all look like we are off to a wedding or cocktail party.

In the flesh, Carl is well over six foot tall with the sort of physique that screams gym sessions and plenty of them. His face is softer and even better looking than his photograph and he has a deep tan suggesting that he's just jetted back from a holiday somewhere warm. He is smiling as he sits down facing Elaine who has suddenly morphed into a nervous looking interviewee. Any minute I'm expecting Carl to cast his eye over her CV and ask where she sees herself in the next three years.

'Right folks, thanks for making it in early this

morning to meet our new editorial director Carl Martin. We'll start with an introduction from Carl and we'll then move on to a discussion about ideas. So over to you Carl.' Elaine shifts back in her seat and I can see that her hand is shaking slightly as she picks up her pen to take notes. A Queen Bee whose carefully planned flight has been thrown off course.

Carl clears his throat in readiness for his big introduction. When he starts to speak I'm surprised by his accent – if you can call it that – which sounds like a mix of south London and mid Atlantic. The kind of accent some rock stars acquire when they've spent a lot of time in America. It's not unpleasant but it doesn't sound quite real either. Already I can see that Kevin will be taking the mick out of that voice in the pub later on.

'Hi folks, I'll keep this bit brief because the thing I'm really keen to hear is your ideas. If you've already searched for my name, and I'm guessing a lot of you have, you'll see that I come from a solid publishing background. Most of my work has been on national magazines in London but I've also spent some time in the United States. With me you'll be getting a real hands-on editorial manager and I'm excited about taking Cornwall Now onto the next stage of its development. My management style, to use that awful term, is informal and I'm looking forward to meeting you all individually afterwards. Now I said I'll keep this brief so I'll be true to my word. So Elaine back to you to kick off the ideas session...' He gives everyone another smile as he glances around to gauge our reaction to his introduction. I catch Kevin's eye as he tries to stay poker faced and I just know he's desperate to laugh out loud. So am I actually.

We spend the next half hour kicking around ideas. Carl doesn't say much but I can see that he's listening intently. When it comes to my turn I can feel my stomach churning as Carl stares across the table. Silly but true.

Guessing that he's the sort who likes to keep things short and simple, I whizz through my story ideas which include a special feature on up and coming Cornish fashion designers. He clearly likes this one and suggests that we could sponsor a fashion show with an award for the best designer.

'That's the sort of idea we need more of' he says smiling over in my direction. 'Ones that can translate into events and showcase local talent. That's a great suggestion Debbie and we'll talk about it more later on.' I can feel myself blushing and daren't even look across at Kevin. Instead I just nod back and mumble a feeble sounding 'thanks'.

Predictably I'm given some good humoured ribbing during our coffee break. I can see Carl is deep in conversation with Elaine and at one point they glance across in my direction.

'Hey teacher's pet, I've rescued a chocolate cookie for you.' Kevin is holding a giant cookie in one hand and a steaming mug of coffee in the other.

'Less of the teacher's pet you' I reply snapping off a piece of the cookie. They've pushed the boat out for Carl's first meeting and have gone for some decent tasting coffee and snacks. Usually we get instant coffee and a few cheap supermarket biscuits thrown in if we're lucky. Already Carl is making his mark.

'Well let's face it you are' Kevin replies winking and nudging my arm. 'Next thing he'll be offering you Elaine's job.' He laughs and takes a big bite out of the cookie while I give him one of my 'piss off Kevin' looks.

'Could I have a quick word with you Debbie?' I spin around to find Carl heading towards us and I hope to God he hasn't heard Kevin's stupid quip. If he has he's showing no signs of it. Out of the corner of my eye I can see Kevin grinning as Carl suggests that we move across to a quieter area of the room.

Closer up I can't help noticing how smooth Carl's skin is with just the beginning of some fine lines around the eyes. Even though I'm wearing higher heels than usual, I'm conscious of the difference in our heights and grateful when he suggests that we take a seat. Already I can feel several pairs of eyes boring into us, not least Elaine's. She's talking to her assistant but is looking directly across at us.

'Debbie, I'd like to hear about more about you and how your work fits into the magazine' he says, staring intently at me. 'I've already read some of your pieces and they are good.'

Again I can feel myself blushing and hope that he doesn't notice. Where to start then? Personal or just work related?

I'm just about to reply when his phone rings out and he glances down to see who it is.

'Sorry Debbie I'm going to have to take this. You stay put – I won't be long.'

As he dives across the room to take his call, I look over to see Kevin smiling and he waves across giving the thumbs up. I also catch Elaine's eye and she looks preoccupied. Somehow I can see that planned girls' night out with her happening a bit quicker than we thought.

'Sorry about that Debbie' Carl says plonking himself back down beside me. 'I'm all ears now.'

Chapter 23

Somehow I've managed to walk home, though I barely remember the journey. My head is still buzzing from this morning's conversation with Carl Martin and his offer of a new role on the magazine.

He's decided to create a new 'event manager' post with selected magazine features linked to a series of live 'road shows'. So features on chefs and restaurants get turned into Cornwall Now sponsored cookery shows and my idea for a fashion talent feature becomes an associated magazine awards show. He doesn't seem to mind that I haven't done this sort of thing before.

'You'll learn things quickly Debbie I just know it.'

His words are still ringing in my ears as I scoop up the latest mound of post in the hallway. I've been given a few days to think it over but it's clear that Carl has already made up his mind. I guess he's a sort of 'my way is the highway' guy and won't easily take no for an answer.

Of course I'd be lying if I said I wasn't flattered by the offer and the opportunity to learn exciting new skills. But – let's face it there is always a 'but' –

it will mean longer and more unsociable hours and more travel. Yes there will be a bigger pay packet and job security but still.....is this really what I want at this stage of my life?

Inwardly cursing the pile of pizza delivery and furniture sales flyers making up most of today's mail, I then spot the official brown envelope which I recognise instantly from my earlier correspondence. It's from the adoption agency, so no question about the contents. This really shouldn't come as a surprise because I've already agreed to receive an introductory letter from my son.

'My son.'

Even thinking those words causes me to catch my breath and I suppose I'm taken aback by how quickly he has responded.

Inside there is a brief note from the agency worker attached to another blue envelope with an air-mail logo at the top. A missive all the way from Canada and I carefully prise it open, trying not to tear the edges. Two photographs tumble out. One is a black and white picture of a boy aged around 7 years old, smiling awkwardly at the camera. The other is a graduation picture, the young man grinning confidently with determined deep brown eyes. My eyes. My dark wavy hair as well. No doubt about it, my son.

I'm reluctant to take my eyes off those photos but still anxious to read the letter He's typed it out but has signed it at the bottom with a flamboyant hand. 'Best Wishes Andy'.

So it's Andy then. Informal like his mum.

'Dear Debbie,

Thank you for agreeing to receive a letter from me. The adoption agency told me that you like to be called 'Debbie' so I hope you don't mind me using the shortened version of your name.

I've been searching for you for some time now and you can only imagine how elated I was to hear that you were happy to accept a letter and some photos. The first picture was taken just after we arrived in Canada and then there's my graduation one from medical school. I'll send you some more recent photos if you want them – my hair has gotten a little greyer now but otherwise I'm still recognisable!

I've thought a lot about what to say but now it comes to writing it down, I'm finding it hard to express myself. So please forgive me if my thoughts come over as a bit muddled and I'll try not to cover too many areas in this first letter.'

I pause to take a deep breath before reading more. I can barely believe that this is for real, that the son I handed over to the adoption workers all those decades ago is reaching out from a place thousands of miles away. Tears are cascading down my face and I carrying on reading through a watery blur.

'I knew I was adopted as a baby. My mom and dad,

Theresa and Joe, told me as soon as I was old enough to understand. I grew up as an only child because they couldn't have any children of their own. I didn't mind really, although I was sometimes jealous of my buddies who had brothers and sisters to squabble and play with.

I'm not sure whether being an only child made me bookish and studious but that's the type of kid I was and mom and dad encouraged it. I got good grades at school but still liked sports, especially baseball and swimming. Toronto has great sporting facilities and I came to love the place. I guess that's why I haven't moved away and I now work as a general medical practitioner right in the heart of the city. I adore my work, (though it has challenges sometimes), but I guess everyone's work is the same. I've got my own place now and have a new girlfriend called Lauren. She's also a doctor and I met her through work. It is still early days in our relationship so I haven't told her about my attempts to contact you and this letter. I'm hopeful that this relationship will last the course and I've already introduced her to mom and dad which is a big deal for me! I live in an apartment just a few blocks away from where I work, so there is no time wasted in commuting and it's a great place for chilling out with Lauren and friends.

I guess you might be wondering what prompted me to try to make contact. I'd been thinking about it for some time but didn't want to tell mom and dad as I thought they'd be hurt. Then I had a seriously ill patient who told me that he had been adopted as a child. His biggest regret was that he hadn't managed to find his real parents and that he might die without knowing who they were.

A few weeks later he did pass away and it made me so sad that he never fulfilled his last greatest wish. So that is why I made the decision to try to trace you – I didn't want to be like that poor man in years to come, not knowing his own true flesh and blood.

Telling mom and dad was one of the hardest things I've had to do but I needn't have worried. They were brilliant about it and said that they'd help out in any way they could. Mom said that she always knew the day would come when I'd try to contact you and she was ready for it. They were told that you were unmarried and aged only 16 at the time and there was no named father on the birth certificate. Between us we managed to make contact with the adoption agency and they agreed to get in touch with you on our behalf. I didn't dare hope that you'd still be around, let alone willing to accept a correspondence from me

It would be just great if we could talk and I've included my telephone contact and email. However, I will understand if you just want to exchange letters to begin with and I can also appreciate how difficult this must be for you. I guess you might have your own family to consider and that you may not have told anyone else about me.

There is a lot to think about but I really do hope we can make further contact in some way. I will sign off now and thank you again for agreeing to let me write to you. It means so much.

Best Wishes,

Andy

Chapter 24

I've lost count of the number of times I've read Andrew's letter and must have spent hours staring at those two photographs. Armed with some basic information, I've searched online but like me he doesn't seem to be a big social networker. So there isn't much more to go on other than the details in his letter. Still, it's more than enough for the time being and it has struck me how complicated my life has become over the past couple of months.

Despite falling into bed dog tired, I haven't been sleeping well and in the early hours of the morning have been trying to weigh up the pros and cons of contacting my son. The pros are the easy bit – finally getting some answers to those nagging questions I've been asking over the years, meeting the handsome and intelligent man I gave birth to and let go. And of course, giving up the secret I've buried for so long. The cons are much greater, far more difficult to grapple with. How can I even begin to tell Amy, my mum and sister? Amy has had so much to deal with in her young life and the thought of causing her more anxiety and pain is too much to bear. Mum and sis will be hurt and shocked to the core as well.

Then there is Mr DJ who in his old age could be about to have his world turned upside down. You see his former girl friend - the very one who has recently got in touch - isn't just an old flame, a name from the past.

No. She also happens to be the mother of the man who he fathered all those decades ago. A pregnancy and a son he knows nothing about.

Of course, there is no need to involve Mr DJ at all. I could just carry on pretending that I don't know who the father is, that it was the result of a hazy and drunken one night stand. Let's face it, nobody would be any the wiser. Then again, this would mean more lies and I have to ask myself why I've *really* got back in touch with Mr DJ? Wouldn't it be better for everyone just to tell the truth, to let Andrew know who his father is and to give Mr DJ the choice of whether to meet him - or not?

So much to think about and that includes the new job offer from publishing big-wig Carl Martin. Although feeling half dead from lack of sleep, I've got a meeting with him later today to give him an answer. Compared to the other conundrum in my life, this one is relatively simple. After all, what's the worst that could happen if I say 'yes'? The extra work and concentration might even make me exhausted enough to sleep through the night – if only.

When I arrive at the Cornwall Now office, praying that I look a bit better than I feel, Carl has a phone clamped to his ear and it looks like the conversation is going to run for a good few more minutes. He signals an apology, raising his eyes to the ceiling and waves across to Sally the magazine's production assistant.

Sally weaves across the room clutching a pile of paper in one hand and a half eaten bagel in the other.

'Sorry Debbie' she says plonking the papers down on a spare desk. 'As you can see he's tied up on a call. Can I get you something while you wait? Hopefully he won't be too long now.'

'No thanks Sally. I'll just pop across to chat to Kevin and you can let me know when Carl's ready to see me.'

Kevin is staring fixedly at his computer screen and looks like he's concentrating hard. He jumps when I tap him on the shoulder but is still pleased to see me.

'Debbie – what a lovely surprise. Wow you look smart today.'

Trying to make up for the lack of sleep, I've made an extra effort with my appearance and have chosen one of my few designer suits topped off with some killer high heeled shoes.

'I've got a meeting with Carl in a few minutes' I

reply, running my hand across by hair. I can see Kevin's eyes twinkling and I can guess what's coming next.

'Ooh – teacher's pet one-to-one then? Wonder what it's about?' He smiles and I return it, not rising to the bait.

'Are you lunching today sir?' I ask, hoping that he will be.

'I thought you said we shouldn't get together again until Sunday? Debbie's rule remember?'

Of course I do, but right now I need my best friend's company.

'Aren't you always saying that rules are meant to be broken? Anyway, is it to be lunch or not? Carl will be off that phone any minute now.'

'Go on then Debbie, twist my arm. Just give me a shout when you've finished with his nibs.'

I don't have time to respond before Sally is waving at me from across the room.

Time to go and see the headmaster then.

Carl looks preoccupied as I gingerly enter his office but quickly replaces his furrowed expression with a big smile.

'Come on in Debbie – sorry about the wait. '

He pulls up a chair alongside his desk which is remarkably tidy for a publication manager approaching press day. There are no piles of paper, photographs or personal knick-knacks. Just functional things and two laptop computers placed side by side. I suppose this shouldn't be too much of a surprise as he's the new kid on the block. It's all a bit sterile and soulless though.

'So Debbie have you thought over my idea for putting you in charge of promotional events?' He is staring hard at me, his eyes showing a steely reserve.

I bet he takes no prisoners, ploughing ahead and always getting his own way. I deliberately wait a few seconds before replying, just enough to unsettle him slightly.

'Yes I have thought about it and I think I'd like to give it a go.'

He gives me a broad smile and makes a thumbs-up sign while glancing across at his computer screen.

'Great stuff, you should always give things a try. That's the sort of attitude I like to see. Now I'd just like to talk you through these ideas....'

I cough before interrupting him in mid flow.

'Er, before we do that, could I just run a few things past you?'

He looks surprised that I've interjected and looks up from his computer screen, cocking his head to one side.

'Go on then Debbie, ask away.'

'Well, I'd just like to know how much travel there will be and what sort of salary I can expect?' I can feel myself reddening but I don't want him to think that he can just steam roller ahead without discussing terms and conditions.

He smiles again before taking another quick glance at his computer screen. I suspect he's waiting for an important email and doesn't want to miss it the second it comes in.

'I was going to come on to that but since you've asked, we'll deal with it now. There will only be travel across Cornwall to start with and obviously you'll get a company car and overtime. I was thinking of a year contract on, let's say, £40,000 plus bonuses if the shows are successful. So how does that sound?'

Compared to my part-time freelance payments, this is a big pay hike and I'm relieved that I'll be getting a car and that the travel will be confined to Cornwall. Although I've also picked up on his words 'to start with.'

'That sounds fine' I answer trying to appear much more nonchalant than I really am.

'Right then, we can sort the ins and outs of the contracts later. Now as for these ideas I've been thinking about...'

He is like a greyhound out of a trap and by the

time I leave his office my brain is spinning. Fashion, art, music and food shows are just for starters. Heaven knows where I'm going to get the energy to keep up with this dynamo.

Kevin is already waiting with his coat on when I come out of Carl's office and immediately spots my beleaguered expression.

'You look like you need a liquid lunch' he quips, taking hold of my arm and giving it a squeeze.

'You're not kidding' I reply. 'But let's go somewhere a bit more swanky than Bits and Pizza.'

Kevin raises an eyebrow and before he has the chance to say anything else, I put my finger to my mouth before whispering 'Ssh - lunch is on me. I'll tell you all about it once we're out of the office.'

As we head across the room I can feel several pairs of curious eyes following us and in the background I spot Carl in an animated conversation with the editor Elaine.

He looks excited while she looks like a deer caught in a headlight.

Stunned and mouth agape.

Chapter 25

'Penhaligans' is a boutique hotel in the heart of Truro and they've made a big deal about bagging a top chef from one of the country's best restaurants. When we get there the place is reassuringly busy, but I manage to get a discreet table at the far corner of the dining room with a view across to the Cathedral.

'This place will set you back a bit Debbie. There's still time to change your mind and we can just go for a pasty and a pint.' Kevin laughs as I roll my eyes and signal across to the waiter that we are ready to order drinks.

'Could we have a bottle of Prosecco and two glasses?' I ask before Kevin has a chance to try to persuade me to go for the cheaper house wine option. The waiter nods and disappears without attempting to sell us some over priced bottled water - a big plus in my view.

'Right then Debbie, what are you celebrating? And you'd better drink most of that wine yourself as some of us have work to do.' He grins and picks up a silver fork to inspect, nodding approvingly.

I quickly fill in Kevin about the details of Carl's offer, telling him to keep schtum about it for now. He's especially impressed with the payment offer which is a fortune in terms of Cornwall Now's usual staff wages.

'It's only for a year contract' I say a bit too defensively, realising that it is probably way higher than his annual salary.

'Still Debbie, you must have made an impression. Seriously though, I'm delighted for you. I take it you've said yes?'

I nod as the young waiter returns with our drinks, expertly opening the Prosecco without causing the contents to cascade out. An art I have yet to master with sparkling wines.

'Here's to our new events manager' Kevin says raising his glass. As our drinking glasses meet, they make a loud clinking sound and we both burst out laughing, me a bit too animatedly. Something I always do when I'm on edge.

After giving Kevin the low down on Carl's plans, we order our food – grilled sea bream for me and a medium rare steak for Kevin. I can feel myself relaxing as the wine takes it effect and true to the chef's reputation, the food is cooked to perfection.

'So how are things with Gilly and the kids?' I ask glancing across at the receding contents of the wine bottle. Why does the fizzy stuff seem to slip down so easily?

Kevin's face clouds over and he gives a desultory shrug, pushing his empty plate to one side.

'Well we had our big talk the other night. It was quite civilised, no shouting or blaming. She just made it clear that she doesn't feel the same about me anymore and said our relationship has become stale.'

'Oh – that must have been hard.' I reach across the table and squeeze his hand. Given what he's just told me there's no sign of emotion in his eyes, just a look of weary resignation.

'When I think back Debbie, all the signs were there. We had just gradually drifted apart, living together more like brother and sister. What with the kids, work and stuff to do on the house. Anyway, she's talking about counselling but I'm not sure....'

I give his hand another squeeze and he smiles across before taking a sip of his wine.

'You should think about it, give it a try at least.' Our lovely waiter gently interrupts us and asks if we'd like to see the dessert menu. I nod, deciding that pudding is a better option than more wine but Kevin says he'll just stick to coffee.

'I just hate the thought of airing our problems in front of a complete stranger. But you're right – we should give it a go especially for the sake of the boys.'

I give him a supportive nod before we put in our

orders for coffee and a slice of blackberry cheesecake for me.

'Have you heard any more back from that old boyfriend of yours?' Kevin asks out of the blue and he immediately catches my shifty glance sideways.

'Hey, you have haven't you? Come on then, what's his latest news?' Kevin is back in mischievous mode and gives me a playful kick under the table.

I want to tell him about my son Andrew, I really do. If I don't talk to someone about it, I'm going to explode. Where to begin though? I can feel the tears welling up and suddenly Kevin's expression changes from amused curiosity to concern.

'What's up Debbie? I was only joking. Jeez what's the matter?'

I'm already fumbling in my handbag for a tissue when the waiter delivers my dessert and our coffees. If he's noticed my distress, he doesn't show it and makes a tactful retreat.

'Listen Kevin, I know you've got to get back to work soon but can you put it off for a bit? I've got something really important to tell you and I could do with some advice.'

Kevin touches my arm before heading outside to call Elaine.

'Don't worry Debbie I'll come up with something – just give me a few minutes and then you can tell me all about it.' After he's gone, I take the opportunity to dab my eyes and smile across at our waiter who is glancing in my direction. I wonder what the poor guy thinks is going on?

I take a few deep breaths, trying to calm myself down before Kevin gets back. Little does he know it, but he's about to be the first person to hear about my long buried secret.

A secret about to explode into the big wide open with God knows what future consequences.

Chapter 26

In the end we spend over two hours at Penhaligans, before Kevin heads back to work with a promise to call around and see me later.

I feel like a massive weight has been lifted from my shoulders and a huge sense of relief. Decades of burying the truth, pretending that I'm a mother to one when I know that I'm living a lie. Not even telling my late husband despite our closeness and deep love. Amy unaware that she has a brother, my mum and sister oblivious to the fact they have a nephew and grand son. Mr DJ with no idea that he also has a son in a far away country. Lies, damn lies, secret familial ties.

When I finally blurt everything out to Kevin he is dumbstruck, hardly able to believe what he is hearing. It is probably only a few minutes, but his silence seems to go on for a long time. Then the practical, clear thinking Kevin kicks in giving some much needed advice.

Get in touch with your son, he suggests. On the phone first and then if that goes well, meet him face to face. Say nothing to Amy for now, just concentrate on seeing Andrew. If, after meeting him,

I want to keep in touch, then tell Amy everything. Follow this with a visit to my mum and sister. Leave Mr DJ out of things for the time being. It's a complication I don't need and that can be a decision for further down the line.

'Small steps Debbie. Take things slowly and one thing at a time.' Sage advice and it all seems to make sense. He's right that I should meet Andrew before saying anything to Amy. She is the one I'm the most scared about telling, not knowing how she will react. We've grown even closer since David died and the thought of anything jeopardising our relationship fills me with deep dread.

'Is it really a price worth paying?' I ask David as we leave the restaurant, emotionally exhausted and all talked out.

'I can't advise you on that Debbie. But I think deep down you know the answer. Otherwise you'll live the rest of your life wondering – what if?'

His words are still echoing in my head when I arrive back home, the answerphone light flashing on the landline phone.

It's probably just a sales call from someone trying to flog double glazing or insurance, damn it. I press down the switch and out comes the soft Liverpool tones of Lil, the adoption agency worker.

'Hi Debbie. Just calling as a follow up to the correspondence I passed on. I thought you might appreciate a chat. You've got my number so feel free to give me a call when you're ready.'

I'm certainly not ready at the moment Lil, far from it. A wave of tiredness washes over me and I'm tempted to just go and lie down for a few hours. I might even get some much needed sleep but I resist the urge, knowing that I'll be awake for half the night if I do. Instead I distract myself with some light gardening in the fading afternoon sun, the rituals of planting and weeding being a welcome distraction.

I'm jolted out of my gardening therapy by the sound of my phone ringing out. This time it's Elaine wanting to arrange 'a girlie night out' to celebrate my new job. So the news is out already then.

'Carl's filled me in and I'm delighted for you Debbie.' Her voice sounds tense though and I guess she's miffed that things have advanced without her knowing about it first.

'It came as a complete surprise to me Elaine but it's an opportunity I can't turn down.' I leave my words hanging in the air, waiting for her response.

'Of course you can't. You'll be great at it and another excuse for us to hit the town. How are you fixed for Saturday?' She's trying to disguise the unease in her voice but isn't succeeding. Somehow I think this girlie night will be more about Elaine letting her hair down and spilling the beans about her real thoughts about Carl Martin.

'Saturday is fine by me Elaine. Shall we meet at

Quills first and take things from there?' She seems happy with that, so we agree to meet up at 7.30pm and I decide that it's time to go back inside before I get collared by old Ted next door.

I must have dozed off because I'm woken up by the sound of the computer telling me that I have a Skype call. It's Amy who has been trying to get hold of me on my mobile and the landline which I'd inadvertently left off the hook after Elaine's call.

'Where have you been mum? I was worried about you.' I can see the concern in her face so I make light of my dodgy hearing and need for an afternoon nap.

'I know you mum. What's going on?' God, if only she knew the whole story.

'Well I have some good news. I was going to call you later but you might as well know now. I've been offered a promotion at work. From next week I'll be Cornwall Now's new editorial events manager.' I watch as her eyes widen and her face breaks into a delighted grin.

'Wowzers mum. That's fantastic. Is it full-time?'

I give her the low down on my chat with Carl Martin and as I'm talking she does a search on his name.

'Mum, he's drop dead gorgeous. Is he your new boss then?'

Amy insists that she must come into the office

with me next time she's home so that she can meet the sexy Mr Martin.

'Tell you what mum. I'll head home the week after next so we can have a celebration and I can check out this new boss of yours.'

I laugh saying that he's much too old for a youngster like her. Oh the bitter irony.

After my chat with Amy, I flick casually through the days post. And there, amongst the usual rubbish, is the latest letter from Mr DJ.

So then - sit down to read and digest his letter or pull out an escapist DVD to watch before Kevin turns up later on?

No contest – the trashy DVD wins hands down.

Chapter 27

True to form, Kevin turns up carrying a huge bouquet of flowers, a box of posh French chocolates and bottle of champagne.

'This lot is to celebrate your promotion and whatever decision you come up with about your son' he announces, tossing his coat into what passes as my cloakroom just inside the hallway.

The flowers are a mix of blooms including white roses. I've always loved roses especially the paler varieties. Somewhere along the line I must have let Kevin know this, unless he's just made a lucky guess.

'These are beautiful Kevin, thank you. I'll dive into the chocolates later on when I've finally digested today's lunch' I say, giving him a peck on the cheek. There's an awkward few seconds when I think he's about to move in for a full on kiss but I pull back in the nick of time. Whatever happens this evening, there is no way Kevin is staying the night. Trust me - this little visit is going to be short and sweet.

'So have you come to a decision yet?' he asks,

tugging at the ring pull on the can of lager I've just got out of the fridge. The champagne will have to wait – it's a good girl mint tea for me this evening.

'Yes I think so' I reply dropping the tea bag into a large mug of scalding water.

'You *think* so?' Kevin asks, eyeing me quizzically. 'Come on, you either have or you haven't.'

'Well alright, I have then. Yes, I'm going to get back to Andrew. I'll tell him a bit about myself first and then we can arrange to talk over the phone.' I wince as I take a sip of the tea which is far too hot. A bit like this topic.

'Good, I'm glad Debbie. I have to admit I'm still reeling from the news and that you've managed to keep it to yourself all this time. It must have been torture.' He's now perched on the small kitchen breakfast chair and looks uncomfortable.

'Lets go into the living room' I suggest, hoping that he hasn't noticed the tears that are welling up in my eyes. Yes it has been tough keeping this to myself but it's amazing how you can hide things, bury stuff and still maintain a sense of normality. We all do it to some extent, it's just that a few people have more to suppress

'Sorry I've foisted this on you at such a bad time in your own life' I say as I flop down on my 'telly watching' chair as I call it, leaving him to sit alone on the sofa. I don't want to risk physical closeness for fear of what it might lead to.

'Come on, that's what mates are for' he replies, smiling across and it is one hell of an attractive smile. I take another swig of mint tea to distract myself.

'Anyway Kevin, it hasn't been all that bad. I've grown used to pretending and after a while it becomes normal. It is only on his birthday or at times like Christmas when I wonder what he's up to, where he is.' I don't want to cry in front of Kevin so I use the excuse of needing the loo to compose myself. Just enough time to save my mascara from running and to calm myself down.

When I get back, I can see Kevin eyeing the upmarket cream envelope I've left lying on the living room table. It has been posted in Beaconsfield and sharp as a pin, Kevin has put two and two together.

'Is this what I think it is?' he asks, examining the neat ink written handwriting.

'If you mean is it from Mr DJ then yes' I reply tartly, grabbing the envelope before he gets the chance to look at it further.

'Thought as much. Quite a delicate hand for a bloke.' He laughs trying to break the ice and suddenly I want him to leave. Incredibly rude I know but true.

'Look Kevin, I hope you don't mind but I'm not really in the mood for any more chatting tonight. All I want to do is finish my tea and go for an early night. Sorry.'

'Sounds like a plan but I assume it doesn't include me?' Before I can answer he puts up his hands in mock surrender. 'Only joking! I'll head off then and just make sure you have a glass of that champers and some chocolate while you're at it.' I promise him that I'll do just that before ushering him back into the hallway to get his coat. As I watch him head towards his car, the tears I've been holding back start to cascade down my cheeks.

It's really far too early to go to bed but I do so anyway, taking Mr DJ's latest letter with me. Kevin is right, he has got quite 'girly' looking handwriting but there is a masculine quality to it as well, someone who seems to be in control and satisfied with how his life has turned out. Let's see what he's got to say this time then.

'Hi Debbie,

I really enjoyed reading your last letter and about the things that have made you the most happy. You seem to have turned into a well rounded person, a long way from the lovely but insecure young woman I recall all those years ago. But we're all uncertain in our late teens aren't we?'

Late teens. Ha, he still hasn't worked out that I hadn't even reached my 16th birthday when we first got together. Just as well I don't put myself out there on the social networking sites with all those visible age and birthday milestones. Still, he can find out if he really wants to and at some time I'll need to 'fess up' as Amy would say.

'So my turn now. My kids make me happy all the time and it's been a privilege to become a dad again later in life. I wasn't around that much when my oldest Lulu was growing up, so I'm enjoying spending more time with the boys. As you know, my work made me happy and now I've replaced it with my hobbies – collecting old jukebox players (I have six!) and my stints as a geriatric DJ in Tenerife.

Talking of Tenerife, I love the place and when the boys are out of school I'm thinking of moving over there lock, stock and barrel. I'll probably keep a smaller place over here to crash in when I'm visiting. I should get a fair price for my place in Beaconsfield when I decide to put it on the market and the money will give me a great lifestyle in Tenerife.

Having financial security makes me happy – I call it my 'fuck off' money, my ticket to live my life as I want to. Money isn't everything, (I'm still an old hippy at heart Debbie), but it gives freedom which IS everything, isn't it?

Now for your theme – regrets. Well to quote the song, I have a few and would have lived a bloody boring life if I didn't. Sadly I regret both of my marriages for different reasons. I neglected my first wife Helen and then work was mainly to blame. I was travelling all over the world, chasing the tails of some top musicians and living their mad hedonistic lifestyle. At that time, I drank too much, took many drugs and partied way too hard. I had a few flings here and there as well. I won't call them 'affairs' as most of them were one or two night stands. But the lifestyle took its toll and my first marriage went the same way when Lulu was only a toddler.

I swore I wouldn't get married again and then met Caroline, who was twenty years younger than me and was working in music PR. She was drop dead gorgeous and bright as well, with a great knowledge of pop music. At first we were head over heels in love and for the first five years things were fine. People commented on the age difference but it didn't seem to matter. Then after the boys were born, she seemed to change. She was unhappy being a stay at home mum and the cracks started to show in our relationship. This time it was her who started an affair, with a man who was nearer to her own age. One day I came home early from work and caught them together. So that was it. A quickie divorce followed with both of us having shared care of the boys. I must admit that I was gutted at the time and went back to drinking too heavily and playing the field. Then I pulled myself together, mainly for the sake of the boys. If it wasn't for them I don't know where I'd be now. Probably an old soak with a dodgy liver!

My other big regret is treating some people badly, betraying them to win work contracts and stealing clients from them. In business it is safe to say that I was no gentleman and I lost a few close friends in the process. That's the name of the music publicity game though, dog eat dog. You just go along with it to survive and only realise what a bastard you were when you finally break free. I hope I'm a much better person now and more loyal *to my good friends.*

Apart from these things, I have few other regrets and I don't spend my life lamenting what might have been. You can't change the past, so what's the bloody point? No, I like to live my life in the moment now. You only have to look at a dog playing on a beach or a child enjoying an ice-cream and you realise that it's the only sane way to live your life. Except when you get to my age, you can't ignore the future and what little time you have left.

So here's my next theme. What will be your next big life adventure? I don't mean that silly interview question 'where do you see your life going in the next 10 years?' shit. No, just where you see your next life destination, a rough map of the future.

That's it for now then and I'm off to play some old fashioned vinyl singles on my juke box. Happy days!

Here's to the next letter,

Peter x x ☺

So my next big life adventure eh?

Well, Mr DJ you've certainly touched on the right theme given what has happened over the past few weeks.

And little do you know what you're really asking.

Chapter 28

I don't know whether it was the after effects of reading Mr DJ's latest missive, or the two large glasses of champagne I swigged down later on. Whatever it was, I've just had the best night's sleep I've had in ages. Uninterrupted, blissful and deep shut eye.

It's amazing how much clearer things seem after a decent sleep. What were seemingly insurmountable problems only a few hours ago, suddenly don't seem all that bad. The sun is shining today as well which lifts my mood and I even manage to give a cheery wave to old Ted next door as I head off on my early morning walk into Truro. If only all days started like this.

Mr DJ's letter has reinforced my decision to reply to Andrew. This time I'll go for email, so there will be a speedy electronic connection. I want to speak to him as soon as possible, to hear his voice and get the measure of his personality. Just thinking about it causes my stomach to flip but there is still an overwhelmingly sense of relief as well. But how to 'pitch' that first approach? Do I keep things short and save most of the detail until our phone call? Or do I prepare him a bit more for what is likely to be an awkward disjointed chat?

I'm deep in thought when I hear someone calling out my name.

'Debbie! Hey Debbie – I thought it was you!'

Glancing across the road, I can see it is Jane, the young woman who bought my house just a few months back.

She is out of breath by the time she has darted across between the busy lanes of traffic wending its way into the town centre.

'How are you?' she asks, huffing and fanning her face. She's wearing a heavy padded jacket which is over the top given this morning's balmy weather.

'Oh fine thank you. Nice to see you' I reply and she notices that I'm staring at her jacket.

'I'm over dressed today – the sun has caught me out!' she says, removing the jacket and draping it neatly over her arm.

After some brief chit chat about how she is settling into my old house and how I'm getting on with my new place, she looks as though she is about to head back across the main road.

'Oh – I nearly forget to say Debbie. We're not that bothered about keeping your old garden shed because we're putting up a summer house. Do you want to have it for old time's sake? Not to worry if you don't but I thought I'd offer.'

The shed, David's other man cave besides the loft. I can see him now pottering about in his old gardening sweater and baggy jeans, ducking in and out of the tiny wooden hut trying to avoid banging his head. I can hear his low whistle and the sound of music from the portable radio he always kept in there.

'Yes, I will if it's not too much trouble for you. It's really good of you to offer.' I give her an appreciative smile which she returns.

'Great. We'll be happy to deliver it to you and it gives me the chance to see your house! Will this weekend be OK?'

We leave things that they will dismantle the shed and drop it over to my place early on Saturday morning. There is a small corner of my garden that I have in mind and it will be useful to have somewhere to put all my outdoor bits and pieces. Of course it will be a fond reminder of David as well, his calming presence in my life. I won't keep it the same fading colour brown though. This time it will have a new lick of pale blue paint and I'll give it a cheeky nautical theme.

How strange that a small piece of David is coming back into my life at such a pivotal time. Some would say it is a sign that he's looking out for me and I'd like to believe that, I really would. But I don't – it's just one of those inexplicable, bizarre coincidences that happen from time to time.

When I get back home, I get straight down to drafting my email to Andrew. It sounds odd 'drafting' an email but this is no ordinary note after all.

'Dear Andy,

Thank you so much for your letter which I received a few days ago and have re-read many times. I'm delighted how well your life has turned out and that you are so settled, happy and successful. I can't deny that it was a real shock to hear that you were trying to contact me but now that I've got used to the idea, I'm pleased that you have made the effort. Over the years I've thought about you, especially on your birthday and other family occasions. But you also need to know straight away that I've never told anyone else about you, not until yesterday when I confided in a close friend. My husband, who died a few years ago, never knew about your existence and neither does my only daughter. One day I hope to explain why I've kept this secret for so long and I hope you'll come to understand. There is so much to talk about and I don't want to go into too much detail in an email. I've got your phone number and I'd like to arrange a time for us to talk. It's bound to be a bit awkward at first but I'm sure we'll be fine. So you now know that I'm widowed and have a daughter. (She is away at university). The rest can wait until our phone call and I'm looking forward to hearing your voice. If you get back to me with a time to call that is convenient for you, I will ring you as soon as I can. I'm a bit nervous about this but excited as well.

All the best,

Debbie.

After saving the email in my draft folder, I pour myself a large black coffee before going back to review it. This is my fourth version and I'm still not entirely happy but damn it, nothing is going to sound quite right in the circumstances. Part of me is tempted to ditch the email and just make that phone call. Then again, he is a busy doctor and is probably doing irregular crazy working hours. Not forgetting the time difference between here and Canada. No, imperfect or not, email it has to be. I press the 'send' button and my note wings its way through cyberspace.

Back in 1975, the thought of being able to communicate thousands of miles across the Atlantic with the press of a computer key would have been incomprehensible. Like all the talk then about robots taking over our lives, or future holidays in space. 'Pie in the sky' as my dad used to scoff. If only he knew what really lay ahead.

Once again my past is about to crash even deeper into the present day. OMG as Amy would say.

Oh My God.....

Chapter 29

It's 8am on Saturday morning and I'm waiting for Jane and her husband Alex to arrive with my old garden shed. I've already cleared the patch of garden where I'd like it to go and the physical work of pulling up weeds stopped my mind from going into overload about the email sent to Andrew.

As things turned out he replied pretty quickly and keeping things short and sweet this time, suggesting that we talk on the phone tomorrow at 12pm UK time. With the shed being dropped off this morning and then a night out on the tiles with Elaine, I have enough to distract me before we finally get to speak. I've decided that I'd like him to do most of the talking, so that I can get a good sense of what he's like as a person - well as much as you can tell over the phone. After that, it will be a question of whether we go to the next big stage of meeting up. Where will that meeting be? More importantly, when? If we do go ahead with a face to face, I'd much rather it was sooner than later.

As I'm pondering all of this, I catch sight of a navy blue transit van pulling onto the driveway. Jane jumps out first and waves to me through the window. She's wearing some loose fitting overalls and her hair is tied back in a pony tail. Without the make up and smart clothes, she could pass for a teenager and her husband Alex looks younger too in his T shirt and jeans. It strikes me that I've only ever seen them both in their office wear and how their formal work clothes make them appear so much older and sophisticated.

After making them both a cup of tea and giving them a quick tour of the house, we set about putting back together David's old shed. Once it's in place, I'm surprised how emotional I feel and yet again I'm trying hard to fight back the tears.

'Oh Debbie before I forget – I found this wedged behind one of the shed panels when I was dismantling it yesterday.' Alex hands me a large brown envelope which is sealed inside a clear plastic bag.

Jane smiles across at her husband.

'I wanted him to open it but he said it might be something private. He's not as nosey as me.'

I laugh and joke that perhaps David had a private money stash which will now come my way. Instinctively though, I don't open the envelope in front of them and it's not long before the couple are reversing off the drive with a plan to head into Truro for a big English breakfast. Oh to be young and have such an uncomplicated life again.

Now I'm alone, I press on the outside of the

package and it feels like a stack of cards. My hands
are shaking as I tear open the envelope and I'm right
– there are five cards. Two of them are birthday
cards – one of them for David's 50th – and two are
Valentine day cards. The fifth one looks like a hand
made one with dried flowers and glitter shaped
hearts.

All are from the same person. Jemma. 'Love you
with all my heart forever' Jemma. 'Until the day we
can be together' Jemma. 'Can't stop thinking about
last night' Jemma. 'So looking forward to our first
holiday together' Jemma. All have kisses and hand
written smiley faces. The words are intimate and
playful, greetings from a lover. His lover.

Suddenly I feel faint and slump down on the
kitchen floor. I can't bring myself to move and just
sit there listening to the kitchen clock ticking. Tick.
Tock. Tick. Tock. Tick fucking Tock. The 'F' word
gets lodged in my mind and I can't get rid of it. Yes
me, the one who hardly ever swears.

An hour passes before I finally drag myself to my
feet, forcing myself to look again at the cards. The
name Jemma doesn't mean anything and I don't
recall David mentioning a work mate by that name.
Her handwriting is big and rounded and the words
make her sound young. 'So looking forward to our
first holiday together.' Was this being planned in
the run up to David's death? I recall that a few
weeks before he died, he mentioned something
about going to Europe on a work project. So had he

been hatching a plot to get away with this Jemma? Then the line 'I can't stop thinking about last night.' Was that written after their first night together? David was frequently on the road, spending several nights a month away from home. He always told me how lonely he was staying in some impersonal mid-priced hotel and eating by himself in his room. When he made those calls back home, was Jemma giggling in the background at the gullible little wifey left behind?

I've read about people who say that they didn't have a clue that their husband or wife was cheating on them and I've always scoffed in disbelief. Surely, there must have been hints that something was amiss, changes in behaviour and demeanour? Well, so much for my smugness and cast iron confidence that my own marriage was rock solid. David – my husband of over 25 years – had been seeing someone else and I hadn't the slightest inkling that it was going on. Even our sex life was good right up until the end, damn it. A sudden vision of David wrapped in the arms of a much younger and probably more attractive woman, causes me to let out a howl and I dig my nails deep into the soft underside of my arm. I watch distractedly as a small trickle of blood wends it way down towards the palm of my hand.

I jump as the phone rings out and then the answer phone clicks on. My voice booms out, confident and friendly, the pole opposite of how I'm feeling right now. 'Hi this is Debbie. Leave a message after the bleep and I'll get back as soon as I can.'

A pause and then the voice of Elaine.

'Hi Debbie, sorry for ringing so early on a Saturday. I'm about to head out on a shopping trip and I just wanted to check if you fancy going somewhere to eat after we've been to Quills? I'd be happy just to eat at Quills if you like but you might have other ideas and as it's a Saturday it would be best to book. I'll be on this number for the next half hour and after that on my moby. Speak soon.'

Christ, am I going to be able to face a night out with Elaine now? I could call her back and make an excuse that I'm not feeling too well. After all, it wouldn't even be a lie. It's not every day that you find out that your much loved husband was actually a cheating bastard on the side. They say that shock is followed by anger and in my case the anger bit has arrived in double quick time. If David were here right now I'd punch him in the face and as for what I'd do with this Jemma woman well....

I toss the cards to one side, deciding that what I need right now is some physical exercise, something to tire me out enough so that I don't have to think. Slapping some blue paint on the shed – his shed - changes it into something different. He would hate the colour and right now that thought pleases me. Fuck you David and your husband snatching whore. This is my den now, a little outside haven which I'll treat more as a summer house.

The routine of painting has been therapeutic and suddenly the evening ahead with Elaine seems more appealing. I call her to say that we'll eat at Quills and that I'm in the mood to get plastered. Then I remember that I have to make the call to Andrew at mid day tomorrow, so I can't get too drunk. Ah well, anything is better than sitting in brooding about what might have been with David and that trollop. Over the next few days I'll use my journalistic skills to try to find out who this Jemma woman is. Someone in David's circle might know her. She might even be working for the same company – I met David in the workplace, didn't I?

After a long scented bath, I decide to make an extra special effort with my appearance tonight. A woman scorned has to hit back and I'm going to do it by glamming up. I've chosen a tight black dress which is just this side of being too short, at least if you are over 25. I've accessorized it with silver high heels and a waist clinching belt. A slick of bold red lip stick finishes things off.

'Wow mum you look fab' Amy says as I answer her regular Saturday night Skype call. 'Have you got a hot date?'

'Not unless you call my editor Elaine a hot date' I reply trying not to let slip how upset I am about finding the cards earlier. We exchange the usual mother and daughter chit chat before I tell her about my transformation of her dad's old shed.

Suddenly she looks sad and asks me if it was upsetting to see the shed again. If only that was the reason for my subdued mood.

'Well have a good time tonight mum, you deserve it' Amy says breezily as we finish our conversation. 'Love you loads'. She blows a kiss across the computer screen and I tell her that I love her too. I remember that's how David and I always used to end our conversations and I for one believed him. More fool me.

Quills is packed as usual and the air is thick with clashing perfumes and aftershaves. Elaine has bagged a seat near the bar and has already bought a bottle of Cava and has filled two glasses.

'Hey Debbie you look fantastic. Have you spent the day in a beauty salon?' I laugh and tell her that no, I've been painting a frigging shed for most of the day.

'You've certainly scrubbed up well. What's this about a shed anyway?' We pass a few minutes with me telling her about David's shed, how I got the offer of having it back and decided to turn it into my own garden hide away. Not a mention of the bombshell that was found inside it. Not yet anyway.

Three glasses of Cava later and I can't hold back.

'Elaine you've had some bastard men in your life haven't you?'

She peers across, taken aback by my out of the

blue question.

'Well, er, yes. You know I have. What's brought this on then?'

I feel strangely calm, as if I'm telling someone else's story.

'This is what's brought it on. Here, take a look at these – they were hidden away inside David's shed.'

I pass over the bunch of cards and Elaine scans them quickly, as if she's looking at a proof of one of the magazine's features. Her face colours as she reads the words and for once she is at a loss how to react. I put her out of her misery.

'This tells me that my marriage, my supposedly secure and happy relationship, was a sham. He was screwing this Jemma behind my back, the lying cheating son of a bitch.' I take a large swig of Cava to reinforce my point. Elaine remains quiet, taking another look at the cards. Then she comes out with a line that hits like a full punch in the stomach.

'Debbie I think I know who this is.'

Chapter 30

Well there's a turn up for the books, not the response I was expecting.

It takes a few seconds for the information to sink in.

'What do you mean you *think* you know who it is?'

Elaine shifts in her seat and looks uncomfortable. She glances down again at the stack of cards as if double checking that she's on the right track.

'I recognise the hand writing and the way of signing off.' She looks across at me with a mix of pity and embarrassment. I just want her to spit it out and my face shows it.

'We had a Jemma Atkins working as a marketing intern a few years ago. You may have seen her around although she wasn't with us for long.' Elaine coughs and takes another sip of her Cava. I'm all ears. All eyes. All everything.

'Go on' I reply, just wanting her to cut to the chase.

'She had just left university and after a few weeks

with us a job came up on the Cornwall Echo for a junior marketing assistant. Jemma asked me if I'd give her a reference and I did. Anyway, she got the job.'

My mind is buzzing. She'd just left university, so would be just a few years older than Amy is now. Bloody hell, can things get any worse?

'When was this?' I ask, trying to stay calm and in control – the pole opposite of how I'm feeling.

'Oh about 5 years or so ago. Anyway, I know David worked in the same department and as I said, I recognise her writing style. She was a real flirt too and had half the men in my sales department drooling every time she walked across the office....' Elaine stops, realising that perhaps she should have left that last bit out.

I can feel my face reddening and I put my hand across the top of my glass when Elaine tries to refill it with Cava. I need my brain to be razor sharp and I make a point of pouring a large glass of water.

Mentally, I'm trying to do the maths. David died three years ago so if Jemma was in her early 20s when she joined his department, he would have been old enough to be her father or at a push grand father. He would probably been her boss too. I'm beginning to feel physically sick and gulp down some water to steady my stomach.

'Are you OK Debbie? Do you need to go outside for a bit?' Elaine looks concerned that I'm about to keel over inside the crowded bar.

'I'll be fine in a moment' I reply, downing some more water. I can see a couple on the next table and they are in that touchy feely early stage of their relationship. I remember when me and David used to be like that with friends telling us to 'get a room' when we became overly tactile. Back then I'd never have believed it if someone had told me that David would no longer be here. Let alone that he would have had an affair with someone so much younger than him.

'So what did she look like – this Jemma?' I ask as the cool water begins to take effect.

Elaine shrugs and wipes the condensation off her wine glass.

'Well pretty in a blonde, fluffy sort of way. She wore lots of make up and was always dressed to the nines. She had a good figure and liked to show it off...' Again Elaine stops mid-description, wanting to check my reaction before continuing.

I try to stay poker faced but can't manage it. Sod it, I'm upset so what's the point of pretending?

'She had a good brain though' Elaine continues 'and she knew she had it all. Looks and the grey matter, a girl who was confident that she'd go far.'

If she was a dummy, I'd feel a bit better. Then again, I couldn't imagine David just going for looks alone. He always used to tell me that he thought he'd won the jackpot with me – a stunning wife who was clever as well. Ha bloody ha.

I'm trying to get the image out of my mind of David and Jemma having sex. Had she discovered all the things that turned him on? The sexy underwear and stockings? The right perfume, music and words? Jeez this is pure torture and I just wish I could press the 'off' button like it was some bad TV programme.

Elaine is still looking concerned and clearly the evening isn't turning out to be the fun one she had planned. She orders another bottle of Cava and heads to the toilets to give me a few moments on my own. While she's away I allow myself a quick slurp of wine and notice that the lovey dovey young couple have slipped away. If only I could turn the clock back to when I was their age, with a matching libido and lust for living in the here and now.

'So do you still want to hang around here or would you prefer that we go somewhere else?' Elaine asks when she gets back a few minutes later.

'Oh let's just stick here' I reply, not wanting to go to the effort of trying to find a table somewhere else on a Saturday night.

'Well I hope you're going to have a bit more wine' Elaine quips, trying to lighten the mood. 'Come on, it'll cheer you up.'

Against my better judgement, I cave in telling myself that I'll be fine by 12pm tomorrow. After all,

I have to be.

As the Cava kicks in, I decide to tell Elaine about Mr DJ as a way of getting the subject off David's affair. But not before making her promise that she'll make some discreet inquiries about where that strumpet, Jemma Atkins, is now working.

'Hey Debbie that would make a fantastic feature' she says after I tell her about my correspondence with my first much older boyfriend. Of course, I haven't mentioned the real reason for contacting him and the fact that I'm going to be talking to our grown up child within the next few hours. Now that *would* be a feature to write but it's not going to happen.

Elaine hasn't picked up on the irony of me contacting an older former lover at the same time as discovering that my deceased husband had been carrying on with a much younger woman.

'Do you think you'll meet up with him?' she asks after I've described his palatial second home in Tenerife.

'I'm not sure. It's still early days but you never know. It would be nice to get away for a holiday in Tenerife if he were to offer.'

I can see from Elaine's face where this is going. She wants a full on reunion in sunny Tenerife with the photos to go with it. A good human interest double spread feature in Cornwall Now. I'd better change the subject before she has me jumping on the next available flight out.

'So how are you getting on with Carl?' I say, helping myself to a slice of cheese from our shared tapas plate, to soak up the alcohol.

Elaine's face clouds over and I can see that I've touched on a raw point.

'Well he's certainly a dynamo but you already know that' she replies, glancing around to check that nobody is close enough to hear our conversation.

'Hmm – I'm a bit worried that he'll expect too much from me. He's taking a risk not having a proper events manager' I say, confiding my own inner doubts.

'Nonsense, you'll be great Debbie. He can see talent and you've got it. It's me who should be worried not you.' Suddenly I can see the vulnerable side of Elaine, the one that she normally keeps well hidden behind the mask of competent magazine editor.

'But why? He needs you at the helm, someone who knows Cornwall and its readers. He can't run the magazine on his own.'

Elaine doesn't look convinced and signals to the waiter that she wants another bottle of wine. She meant it when she said earlier that she wanted to get wasted and has already polished off the best part of two bottles of Cava on her own. Despite the shock of earlier today, I'm actually pacing myself quite well alternating small sips of wine with mineral water.

'I'm going to make a prediction right now' she announces when the third bottle arrives.

'This time next year I won't be the editor and that you'll be shacked up with that Mr DJ of yours.'

She raises her glass for a toast and although we laugh, neither of us is doing so for real.

If the eyes are a window to the soul, we've both got the shutters firmly down.

Fake laughter matching our dummy bonhomie.

Chapter 31

I'm surprised to find that I've slept reasonably well after yesterday's bombshell discovery and the night out with Elaine. We finally called it a day at pub closing time when I bundled Elaine into a taxi and cleared my head by walking home. I then hid the stash of cards behind some office files before re-reading Andrew's first email to me. Eventually I must have nodded off without setting the alarm clock and woke just after 9am desperate for a glass of water.

Now I'm trying hard not to look again at Jemma's cards or to torture myself with images of them together. Easier said than done though, so I set about studying a map of Canada and a Google shot of the street where Andrew lives. The houses are set well apart and it's a prosperous looking area. I can see the health centre where Andrew works, the local grocery store and restaurants. There are people walking along, their faces blurred and I wonder if one of them is Andrew. Unlikely but you never know.

As the clock nudges nearer to 12pm, I decide that it's time for me to jot down some questions. It might sound odd doing this for a first raw chat with my own flesh and blood, but the ritual of preparing for an interview – and that's what it is really – is comforting. My first questions are all about him, his adopted family and life in Toronto. My follow up ones are more difficult. How does he feel about me abandoning him at such a young age? Does he understand why I did it? Then the anticipated questions from him to me. The most difficult – do I know anything about his father? Why have I kept it a secret from my own family for so long? And the really big one - am I prepared to meet him in the flesh?

As the clock hand approaches 12pm I can feel my stomach churning and my palms getting clammy. I have the phone number in front of me even though I know it off by heart. Out of the corner of my eye, I can see old Ted outside pottering in his garden, going through his Sunday ritual of weeding. He stops to look at my brightly painted shed, cocking his head to one side like a blackbird listening out for a worm. Doubtless he'll be giving me his opinion of it later, telling me it's a funny choice of colour for a shed.

A deep breath and I start to dial the number, my heart pounding. Then that voice, my son's voice, which I'm hearing for the first time.

'Hello Andy speaking…'

For a few seconds I'm lost for words, dumbstruck as they say.

'Hello – Debbie is that you?'

The mention of my name propels my brain and mouth into action.

'Yes it's me Andy. Sorry I'm just a bit nervous that's all. How are you?'

His turn to be silent for a few moments, taking in the sound of my voice.

'Fine Debbie. I'm so glad you called. If it helps, I'm really nervous too. I didn't sleep last night thinking about this call. It's great to hear your voice...'

'Yours too' I reply, trying not to go into emotional melt down. Another awkward silence before we both try to talk across each other. This breaks the ice with Andy quipping that it's probably best if we take things in turns.

His voice is soft with an understated Canadian accent, if there is such a thing. Sing song but in a soothing sort of way and I can hear that he'd be great at reassuring worried patients.

'You are not going to believe this but I spent some of this morning writing down some questions to ask you' I say, adding that my journalistic training had taken over.

He pauses for a moment, taking in the fact that I'm a writer. Of course, there is so much to tell him and he doesn't even know my married name yet, so he won't have been able to do an online search.

'Oh so you're a journalist?' He sounds surprised, bemused even.

'Yes, I trained as a news reporter but now I do some feature writing for a Cornish magazine. ' I think about mentioning my new full-time job offer but decide to leave it for now. We need to take things slowly with a lifetime to catch up on.

'Wow – do you write under your own name?'

'Well yes, my married name – Debbie Mckay. But hey, enough about me for now, I've got all these questions to ask you first.'

Andy accepts this and I ease into my interviewing role. It's easier to pretend that I'm doing this for a feature, to put on my professional hat. Except that I'm feeling as far from professional as you can possibly get and I'm sure that he must be able to hear my heart racing.

I start by asking about his adopted family, his mum and dad. He is clearly fond of them and is keen to emphasise how supportive they have been about him getting in touch with me.

'Mom and dad are just great Debbie, the best ever. If you get to meet them you'll see what I mean.'

I stay quiet, not wanting to interrupt and he quickly fills the space.

'Debbie I know how difficult this must be for you but believe me, I had the best childhood ever and I was lucky that they chose me..' He tails off, waiting for me to respond.

'I'm so happy for you Andy, I really am. You can't believe how difficult it was for me to give you up but I was only 16 and living miles away from home. I didn't tell any of my family that I was pregnant and gave birth alone in the mother and baby home.'

I can feel myself welling up but I need to hold everything together. If I start crying now, it will open the floodgates and it will be impossible to continue our chat.

'I understand Debbie. No mother gives a child up easily and things were much harder back then I guess. The main thing is that we've now made contact, it's all that matters.' I can hear his voice crack slightly and it's all I can do to stop myself from sobbing.

I shift the conversation first to his girlfriend and then to his job, telling him how impressed I am that he's a doctor. We're both more comfortable with the less emotional stuff for now and I listen intently as he tells me all about the lovely Lauren who he thinks is 'the one' and his work at the health centre.

'Now Debbie, come on I need to hear a bit more about you' he says shifting the conversation back to my world.

'Well you know what I do for a living' I reply 'and you know that I have a daughter, Amy, at university. She's studying English Literature at Bristol.'

'Yes, so I have a half sister – I've always wanted a brother or sister' he says sounding excited.

'I haven't told Amy about you yet' I respond trying to play down the note of panic in my voice. 'I didn't tell her dad either. He died three years ago not long after his 50th birthday.'

'Sorry Debbie, I realise that you haven't told any of your family and that I shouldn't get ahead of myself by saying I've always wanted a sibling. It's just my nerves taking over now that I've finally gotten to talk to you. Your poor husband dying at such a young age...' His voice trails off as he waits for me to tell him what led to David's death.

We spend the next few minutes discussing how hard it has been for me to be widowed at such a young age and for Amy to lose her dad. He is so easy to talk to that I forget all about my pre-prepared questions and just let the conversation take its natural course. Then the inevitable, the decision about how to proceed after today.

'Debbie, I'd love to meet if that is OK by you. I'm due to be at a medical conference in London next month and could stay on an extra few days....' Again his voice tails off, waiting for my reaction.

Next month. London. I'd told myself that if we met I wanted it to be quick – no long drawn out wait. Well once again David's favourite expression springs to mind.

'Be careful what you wish for'.

'Of course I'd love to meet you' I reply before I give myself the chance to dither over the decision.

I can hear the happiness and relief in Andy's voice.

'Fantastic – I'd be happy to travel to Cornwall if that suits you better.'

That one I'm not sure about.

'Let me have a think about it and I'll get back to you' I say, my mind buzzing at the prospect of seeing Andy.

We've already been on the phone for over an hour and the conversation was a lot easier than I expected. Thank God he hasn't asked me yet about his father and whether I have an idea who it is. We leave things that we'll speak again in a few days time and he promises to look up some of my articles.

It's only after I've put the phone down, that the emotional impact hits me for six. I let out a deep sob and I'm not sure what I'm really crying about. Tears of joy for finally being reunited with my son? Or sadness that my seemingly perfect marriage was actually anything but?

The answer of course is both.

Chapter 32

After I calm down, I decide to call Kevin to see if we are still on for a promised long walk and pub lunch. I've deliberately steered clear of him for a few days but now I really need to confide in him about my phone chat with Andy.

He sounds half asleep when he answers the phone and I joke about him being the classic lazy weekend guy on his own.

'How do you know I'm on my own?' he quips, adding that he's been in charge of the two boys overnight and they've worn him out.

'So do you still want to go out for that walk and lunch later?' I ask, hoping for all the world that he does. The thought of spending the afternoon on my own doesn't appeal.

'I'm on if you are' he says. 'Where do you fancy going?'

We decide on a country pub just a few miles outside Truro which has a good walk across some nearby fields. It's been raining off and on, so I dig out my walking boots and waterproof trousers. Having lived in Cornwall for most of my adult life, I know that you have to go on a walk prepared for whatever the weather will throw at you.

Kevin arrives at 2.30pm on the dot as we arranged. He's happy to do the driving and we manage to find a place in the crowded pub car park before heading out on our walk. We laugh as we spot a young woman trying to clamber over a rickety wooden stile in a box fresh pair of sparkly trainers. Her boyfriend isn't wearing sensible walking shoes either and is cursing at the muddy ground.

'Got to be visitors' Kevin scoffs, pulling a silly face and imitating the young man's scowl. We march ahead of them feeling virtuous and in the know.

'By the way, I spoke to Andy earlier' I announce and for a moment Kevin has to think who the hell I'm talking about.

'You know, my son Andy.' I add, still not accustomed to using those words.

'Oh God, sorry Debbie. I wasn't expecting things to happen so quickly. How did it go?'

We're walking briskly and I can feel myself getting out of breath. But I don't want to slacken the pace.

'OK I think, not as bad as I thought it would. We're going to meet up when he's in London next month.'

Kevin stops in his tracks turning to face me head on.

'Bloody hell Debbie, you don't hang around. Wouldn't it be better to take things a bit more slowly?'

'No' I snap back, irked by his reaction. 'What's the point of hanging around? He seems lovely, easy to talk to and he's visiting London in a few weeks time. It makes perfect sense to meet him while he's in this country. I thought you'd be pleased for me.'

Kevin looks away briefly before throwing his arm around my shoulder.

'Of course I'm pleased for you. It's just, you know, all of a bit sudden.' He smiles before enveloping me in a big bear hug. I snuggle up to him and for a few minutes we don't move, enjoying the physical closeness.

When we get walking again, I go over the phone call with Andy and for once Kevin doesn't say much. He's listening intently though, taking in all the details.

'So you're sure about the decision to meet him in London?' he asks after I'm all talked out.

'Absolutely. One hundred per cent. In fact I'm really looking forward to it and we're going to have some more chats over the phone before then. I don't want to use Skype because I want to see him for the first time properly – not through a computer screen.'

We walk in silence for a few minutes, our boots squelching on the wet grass.

'Would you like me to go with you Debbie?' The question comes out of the blue as he pushes his hands deep into his jacket pocket. It has started to drizzle and I can feel the temperature dropping.

'What – you mean to London?' I'm taken aback and I pull up my coat hood to shield myself against the light rain.

'You might need someone to talk to afterwards – once you've met Andy. It's not like you can talk to anyone else about this, is it?'

He's right of course and it's a kind offer.

'Thanks Kevin, I'll think about it. Look, shall we head back to the pub before this rain gets worse?'

We walk back in virtual silence, the sort of comfortable silence that you can only have with close friends or relatives. The couple we saw earlier, with the inappropriate shoes, are in front of us now having decided to turn back well before we did. They appear to be arguing and he is marching ahead of her, his stiff posture no doubt echoing his bad mood. I expect they'll be making for the pub like us.

Once inside, we order a roast beef Sunday lunch and I have a large glass of red wine. Kevin orders a pint of lager shandy as he's driving.

We are seated near the pub's wood-burning

stove and the smell of damp wood mingles in with the scent of various cooked meats and vegetables. The hallmark of the classic British pub on a busy Sunday and it could be anywhere in the country.

'I've got something else to tell you Kevin' I say once we're settled into our seats and have inspected the pub in vain for the warring couple in the silly walking shoes. Perhaps they've gone home in a huff, muddy boots and all.

'Go on then' Kevin replies, glancing across at a groaning plate of food that has just been delivered to the next table. An gigantic Yorkshire pudding is sitting precariously on the top of the plate, like an oversized hat.

'Yesterday I had my old garden shed – David's shed – delivered by the couple who bought my house. They didn't want it and asked me if I'd like it. I wish I'd said no now....'

Kevin looks across quizzically and before he can say anything else, I come right out with it.

'There was a package hidden in the shed, the couple found it and handed it over to me. It was a load of cards – birthday cards, a Valentine's card – all of them for David. They were from a woman called Jemma...turns out he was having an affair Kevin. A bloody affair.'

Kevin's mouth is agape and he grabs hold of my hand across the table.

'Bloody hell Debbie. Jeez....' He squeezes my hand and again I'm reluctant to let go.

'Yes, so much for my fairy tale marriage. Elaine thinks she's knows who this Jemma woman is – she might still be working for the Cornwall Echo but she was an intern on the magazine a few years ago.'

I can see the penny drop as Kevin also realises who she is.

'Jemma... Atkins? Christ Debbie she was a youngster, just out of college.'

I remove my hand from his and take a large sip of wine. I can feel my face reddening, a combination of heat, alcohol and the painful reminder from Kevin about just how young Jemma was - and still is.

'Elaine is going to check if she's still working at the newspaper. If she is, I want to meet her, give her back those cards, throw them back at her the slapper...'

Kevin's face is a mix of sympathy and concern.

'Don't do anything rash Debbie. You've got enough on your plate with all this Andy business and God knows, that's enough to deal with. I'd leave things for a while until you get over the shock.'

As usual, he's right and I shouldn't do anything until I've calmed down. Revenge is a dish best taken cold as I've often said myself. Yes well, it's a bit different when it's you at the centre of the storm and a blistering hot dish is the more appealing option.

Talking of which, our food arrives before I get a chance to reply. Suddenly I don't feel hungry and both of us stare at our giant plates of food as if they were something from outer space. Flying saucers topped with meat and gravy.

We make a half-hearted stab of eating but we're both too distracted and push the plates to one side. A passing waiter asks us if everything is OK and I tell her that we made the mistake of having a big breakfast earlier. She smiles, obviously not believing us and politely takes the plates away.

'Let's just go home' I suggest, downing the last few dregs of my wine.

As we make our way back to the car, Kevin puts his arm across my shoulder drawing me towards him.

'I've got something to tell you too Debbie. Me and Gilly are getting divorced. It's all over for us.'

As I turn towards him, he plants a kiss on my lips and this time I return it, revelling in the intimacy.

Anyone looking out of the pub window would see a middle-aged couple in a loving embrace. And in some ways they are not far wrong, except we're just good friends.

Aren't we?

Chapter 33

Kevin stayed the night at my place and we sat up well into the early hours just talking. Yes - *talking*. He poured his heart out about the divorce and his fears about the effect it will have on the two boys. I spoke more about my decision to meet up with Andy and my dread about how Amy would react, should I finally choose to tell her. I steer clear of mentioning Mr DJ and with so much else going on, he doesn't even appear on our radar.

Exhausted, we finally fall into separate beds with me sleeping in Amy's room and I set the alarm for 7.30am as we both have to get up for work. I've got a meeting with Carl at 10.00am to discuss the ins and outs of my new job which starts next week. Afterwards, I'm due to speak to Elaine to see if she's got any more information on the whereabouts of that husband snatching cow, Jemma.

In the end, I wake much earlier and decide to get up rather than battling to get back to sleep. There's no sign of Kevin, so I make myself a cup of tea and head into my little home office. Suddenly the time feels right to reply to Mr DJ's latest letter and, for all I know, this could be my last one to him. After all, if

I do decide that I want a long term relationship with my son, I'm not sure how Mr DJ will fit in or whether I'll ever let him know that he is Andy's biological father.

'What will be your next big life adventure?' As I re-read his last letter, I smile at the irony of his chosen subject but first I have to go over my own theme of regrets. Hells bells, where to start?

'Hello Peter,

It's my turn to apologise for taking so long getting back to you. A lot has happened over the past few weeks and I'm struggling know where to start. Anyway here goes....'

With pen in mid-air, I stop and listen for any sign of Kevin stirring. If I'm going to do this now, the last thing I need is for him to barge in. The house is silent, so I take a deep breath before continuing.

'My first piece of news - the good bit - is that I've been given a new job on the magazine as an events co-ordinator. It means that I'll be organising competitions and road shows and it will be a full-time job. I was offered it out of the blue by our new manager, a guy called Carl Martin. If you do a search on him, you'll see that he's a big name in publishing and he wants to shake things up at Cornwall Now. It's exciting but daunting too and I've got a meeting later to find out what my first big assignment is. So I'll be much busier and travelling around the county in my new company car. Amy is delighted for me and has told all her mates about her mum's 'really cool' job.

My next piece of news is a bit more shocking....'

Another pause as I mull over the wisdom of telling him about my discovery that David was having an affair. Then again, why should I hold back when he has told me about his own wife's affair?

'I discovered a few days ago that David had been having an affair just before he died. I won't go into all the details about how I found out but the documentary evidence is there. Two of my friends know her and she is young enough to have been David's daughter. So the perfect marriage I thought I had – the fairy tale – turns out to be a sham. There they were, plotting holidays and for all I know even a longer term future together. I've read her cards to him and they are intimate, full of gushing detail about their supposed love for each other. I can't get the images of them together out of my head and I'm planning to meet up with this woman – she's called Jemma – to find out more. I know it might seem pointless now that David isn't here but I still need to know how long it had been going on, what led up to it. You'll understand having gone through the same thing with your second wife. I haven't said anything to Amy and she'll be devastated if she finds out – her dad was her hero and still is. Anyway, I chose the theme of regrets last time and now I'm left with the feeling that somehow I must have neglected my marriage, taken David too much for granted. Why else would he decide to have an affair? It's too late to ask him but I do regret not talking to him more, taking weekends away just to be on our own. I had absolutely no idea that this was going on and there were

no clues from David's behaviour. Then again, I wasn't looking I suppose.

Other regrets? Like you I have a few but the shock of this latest news means that I don't want to dwell on them now.

Another pause again as I hear the toilet flush in the distance, followed by light foot steps and the bedroom door closing. Kevin has gone back to bed and I suspect he won't emerge until I wake him up. As the house falls quiet again, I continue.

'As for your theme of my next big life adventure, well what can I say in the circumstances? The shock of David's affair has made me realise that I need to think long and hard about where I'm heading in this new stage of my life. A year or so down the line, once Amy has left university, I might take some time out to travel, meet new people and savour different cultures. There's someone I know in Canada who I'd really like to see and perhaps I could even visit you in Tenerife? Certainly I can see travel featuring big time in the near future.'

It's my turn to suggest a theme for the next letter and the one that immediately comes to mind is 'secrets', a subject I'm an expert in. Is there something that he's hidden from everyone and if so, is he brave enough to share it with me? It's a huge ask, especially given what I've hidden over the years. The reference to someone I know 'in Canada' is me trying to let a glimmer of the truth out. Pathetic I know but if I ever do tell him the truth about Andy, at least there is this 'hint' written down in a letter. Besides, who really knows if this correspondence will ever go any further? Caution to the wind then…

'Anyway, I'd like our next theme to be secrets. Is there anything you can share with me that you haven't told another soul? You'll have to trust me on that one and I'll need to think of a secret that I can confide in you about….'

I laugh out loud at this last line, loaded as it is with bitter irony. Lordy, Mr DJ, if only you could read my mind.

'So there you have it and over to you now. Apologies if this letter has been less upbeat than our previous ones but I know you'll understand.'

Debbie x

Chapter 34

I'm three weeks into my new job and I have to admit that I'm enjoying it. The hectic pace has meant that I haven't had too much time to angst about my meeting with Andy. We've had the occasional quick chat over the phone and so far we've kept things light, both of us knowing that there is some heavy stuff to face when he gets to London.

I've known for some time that Jemma is still working for the Cornwall Echo and is now in a more senior marketing role. I've tracked down her picture on the company website and she is pretty but not nearly as glamorous as I'd imagined. She also looks older than her years but that might be the formal way the photograph has been taken. So far I haven't plucked up the courage to confront her, taking Kevin's advice to leave things alone for the time being. Now that I'm working in events, we could well bump into each other and the mantra that revenge is 'a dish best taken cold' now has a certain attraction. A few nights ago I had a dream that I met her at a drinks party thrown by my boss Carl. She was flirting outrageously with him and when Carl introduced her to me I smiled saying 'Ah yes, the woman who was screwing my husband.' Her face turned bright pink but I woke up before I could launch into a full scale tirade.

Kevin and I have become even closer over recent weeks, confiding in each other and meeting up more often after work. The other night Kevin even quipped that we are becoming like an old married couple and we both laughed - a bit too loudly.

'So how would you feel if we were actually to become a couple?' he asked as we walked back to our cars.

I was too stunned to answer.

'Shall I take that as a no then?' I could see that he was stung my silence after he had finally plucked up the courage to raise the question.

'Er, not necessarily' I replied awkwardly, looking away from him.

It was his turn to stay silent, waiting for me to fill the void.

'It's just that there is so much going on at the moment and while I love having you as a friend, I'm just not ready for anything more. Not yet anyway.' Although it might not have been the answer he wanted, at least it wasn't an outright no.

'OK, I'm a patient kind of guy' he said squeezing my arm.

We continued in silence for a few minutes before I broke the ice by suggesting that I take him up on his offer to accompany me to London.

'Brilliant, I think you're making the right decision' he replied before we exchanged conveniently distracting banter on train times, hotels and how he'd manage to get the time off work. I had already told Carl about some 'family business' I needed to attend to in London and it would mean taking a couple of days off. Given that I'd only just taken on the job, he was surprisingly relaxed adding that he might have to pay a visit to 'The Smoke' himself soon.

All that was a fortnight back, and here I am packing a suitcase for my momentous trip tomorrow. Kevin has already arranged to meet me here at 9.30am before we set off to the railway station. We're both staying in the same hotel in adjoining rooms and have made plans to go out to dinner tomorrow evening, ahead of my big assignation with Andy the following day.

Andy has suggested that we meet at his hotel in Soho and then perhaps go somewhere for lunch. He has booked a small meeting room which will give us complete privacy and we've both promised to bring more photographs of our families. Up to this point I haven't had time to get nervous but now I'm starting to get a serious case of butterflies in my stomach. I've spent hours deciding what to wear, finally opting for a simple silk dress and jacket.

Elegant and understated seems like the best bet and I'll keep my jewellery to a minimum.

I'm still wearing my wedding ring despite finding out about David's affair, although heaven knows there have been times when I wanted to yank it off. Somehow though, I feel bare without it and I'd have to explain its absence to Amy as well. So there it remains, a Cornish gold band inscribed on the underside with the words 'for the love of my life'. Just as well the miniscule inscription is hidden away from the outside world.

I'm woken abruptly by my alarm clock, surprised that I've managed to get any sleep. My stomach is protesting noisily after I didn't eat much yesterday, so I grab a slice of toast as I cast an eye over my emails. Andy has sent a message wishing me a good trip down, adding that he 'can't wait to meet me.' So far I haven't said anything about Kevin, so he's assuming that I'm travelling alone. He is aware though that I'm having dinner with a friend tonight, adding that he hopes 'we have a great catch up.' Suddenly it's all very real and yet again I can feel the butterflies flitting around deep inside my tummy.

We've treated ourselves to outrageously priced first class rail tickets and have a virtually empty carriage. There is one elderly man sitting a few seats away who is studiously reading a copy of the Telegraph, only coming up for air when there is an offer of a complimentary drink or bite to eat.

'So are you still nervous about tomorrow?' Kevin asks once we've opted for coffee and bacon rolls.

'Of course.' I reply glancing out of the window as we leave behind the exquisite Cornish countryside. 'It would be odd if I didn't feel anxious.'

'I'm sure it will all go well' Kevin replies, taking my hand across the table. We stay holding hands for a few minutes before we are interrupted by the cheery ticket collector, whistling under his breath.

'Travelling for business or pleasure?' he asks us as he glances at our tickets.

'A bit of both' Kevin quips and I swear I spot a wry smile exchange between the two of them.

'Well enjoy the trip' the collector adds before moving on disturb Mr Telegraph reader.

It's a tiring journey and I'm relieved when we finally arrive at our hotel. We've opted for a mid-priced one in Islington, close to the Upper Street bars and restaurants. It's also handy to get to Soho where I'll be meeting Andy tomorrow at 10.00am. The rooms are better than we expected, with queen-sized beds and good sized flat screen TVs.

'Do you mind if we just go for a quick meal tonight?' I ask Kevin once we've settled into our rooms. 'I'm a bit pooped and it would be great just to crash out later and watch some trash TV.'

We head for a local Spanish restaurant and end up sharing some delicious tapas. Kevin has a few glasses of red wine but I stick to mineral water, wanting a clear head for tomorrow. We steer clear of talking about Andy and pass the time by making up silly stories about the other diners. 'She looks like a teacher, he's obsessed with tooth picks so he could be a dentist' sort of thing. It's just a light, easy early evening out and when we finally say goodnight, I'm ready for a couple of repeats of one of my old favourite TV shows 'Friends'. Again, nothing too hard on the brain, just escapism at its best.

But I don't sleep well, despite the comfy bed and light TV watching. It's 3.00am and once again I'm back in the moment I handed over Andy to the adoption worker. Aged 16, a mere child myself and desperately alone in a strange town. Another long dark night of the soul looms ominously ahead.

Chapter 35

I've been up since 7am and unable to face breakfast at the hotel, I've made my way across to a little coffee bar just a stone's throw from where I'm due to meet Andy. I've bought a newspaper but can't get beyond a quick scan of the headlines. My watch says it's only 9.00am and I'm tempted to ring Kevin but I'd hate to wake him if he's still in a deep sleep. I flinch as my phone rings out and it's good old Kevin – I'm convinced we've got some sort of telepathy thing going.

'Ah – I was just thinking about calling you,' I say, laughing at the coincidence.

'I got your note,' Kevin replies sleepily 'I've only just woken up. Had the best sleep in ages. How about you?'

'Bloody awful, didn't sleep a wink. I'm throwing coffee down my throat to make sure I don't keel over later on.'

'Where are you Debbie?'

'In Soho. I thought I might as well wend my way over rather than hang around the hotel, getting more and more nervous. Hope you don't mind.'

Kevin pauses and I can hear a knock on the hotel door.

'Hang on a mo Debbie, just need to get this.'

He's ordered room service and I listen as he exchanges some polite banter with the waiter.

'Sorry about that. I didn't want to sit in the restaurant on my own like some saddo so I ordered breakfast to be sent up. I've gone for the full English and sod the cholesterol.'

'Well you'd better crack on with it before it gets cold.' I wish I could face something to eat myself but I'd probably throw up.

'I will then and it'll all be fine Debbie, you wait and see. I'll be thinking about you.'

'Thanks Kevin and before you start stuffing your face, what are your plans for this morning?'

'I'll go for a long walk to burn off some of the breakfast calories and then I fancy a trip to Tottenham Court Road to see what gizmos I can buy. I'm thinking of changing my laptop and there are some good sales on.'

'Well enjoy and I'll call you when I can.'

The coffee bar is filling up quickly and a member of the staff has started to put some chairs outside. A young woman is balancing her coffee cup with a bulging briefcase and asks if it OK for her to sit by me.

'Of course' I reply politely, inwardly hoping that she won't try to make conversation. I smile briefly before pretending to read my newspaper.

'Sorry for interrupting but are you local to London?'

She has a foreign accent but I can't quite place it. It sounds vaguely Swedish but to my untrained ear it could be Danish too.

'No I'm just visiting' I reply crisply, not wanting to sound over friendly.

'Oh, I'm trying to work out how long it will take me to get to Kensington from here.' She obviously hasn't picked up my hint that I'd rather not talk.

'Sorry, I can't really be of help. You could ask one of the staff here, they're bound to know.'

'Yes, good idea. I'll wait until they are a bit less busy. So where are you from then?'

Oh here we go. I can see that come what may she wants to chat but it's too early for me to get up and leave. Besides, I still have a full pot of coffee to get through.

'I live in Cornwall, a city called Truro. It's a long way down in the South West.' For the first time I notice how attractive she is, bright pale blue eyes, striking blonde hair and a classic rosebud mouth.

'Truro you say? I've not heard of it before. I'm from Copenhagen.' She smiles broadly and I can't help smiling back.

After some initial chit chat about Truro, her own home city and the perils of getting around London, I ask her what she does for a living.

'I'm a family lawyer – I specialise in fostering and adoption.' If she notices the shocked look on my face, she's far too polite to say anything.

This is a conversation I really don't want to get in to, so I feign a shocked glance at my watch adding that I really must dash or I'll be late for an important meeting.

'Here's my card if you are ever in Copenhagen' she says as I quickly gather up my stuff. Jeez I can barely get out of the shop quick enough and have to be reminded by the server to pay my bill. I leave an extra large tip by way of apology.

'Cristina de Keyser' it says on the card with a lot of letters after her name. I quickly shove the card in my bag and even though it's only 9.30am, I make my way across to the hotel where Andy has arranged for us to meet. Despite its modest exterior, this is a classy establishment and a doorman greets me as I enter the lavish reception area.

'I'm a little early for my appointment, so could I order a coffee while I wait?' I ask the immaculately turned out receptionist.

'Of course madam. What sort of coffee would you like?' She reels off a huge list of options but as she does so my eyes freeze. It's him, Andy. He's standing by the lift, deep in conversation with someone. It's definitely him. Tall, slim and in the flesh shockingly like Mr DJ at his age.

'Are you all right madam?' The receptionist's voice cuts in suddenly, making me jump.

'Er, sorry – yes. Listen forget about the coffee for now. I've just spotted someone I know.'

Within seconds, I'm standing right behind him. I can hear his soft Canadian accent as he is talking to a young woman about the room hire. Something about not wanting to be disturbed and that we might need the room for this afternoon as well. After they've finished talking, the young woman heads off, leaving Andy waiting by the lift door.

'Andy?'

He spins around and for a few seconds we just stare at each other, unable to say a word.

Chapter 36

As you can imagine, I've read all sorts of things about how people react when they meet their birth children for the first time. Ever since I decided to make contact with Andy, I've made it my business to read about other peoples' reunion experiences. There's plenty out there if you scout around, some with happy outcomes and others ending in disappointment and tears. Almost everyone describes the need to just stand and stare for a while, to take in the face and form of your long lost child, mother, father or sibling. There's a deep-rooted need to explore the features, to see the physical aspects of yourself reflected in the person standing before you. It goes beyond words, like pre-verbal toddlers eyeing each other up.

I don't know how long we've been standing here just staring. The thing that strikes me most, and something that I haven't picked up from seeing his photograph, is the striking resemblance to Mr DJ. The hair texture is identical and so is his nose and mouth. I suppose I've been fixated with his eyes - an identical copy of my own eyes - to the exclusion of everything else. Yet now we are face to face, there is no doubting it. Andy is his father's boy.

'Debbie - wow - it's really you. How incredible to finally meet you.' Suddenly his arms are around me and I'm breathing in his scent. Light woody aftershave mixed with floral soap and his smart cotton shirt still slightly damp from the morning rain.

When I do manage to blurt out my first few words, it's an apology for being early which is pretty pathetic really. He's hanging on to my every word though, and I can see that his eyes are already misting over. In my mind I've rehearsed this moment over and over, fully expecting to be in floods of tears by now. Yet here I am, just about managing to stay dry-eyed and inwardly kicking myself for sounding like a bloody idiot.

'No I'm glad you are early – really glad,' he replies and I can see that like me, he's making a mammoth effort not to cry. Then another few minutes of staring back at each other before he takes hold of my hand, gently squeezing it and this tiny physical gesture is all it takes to send me over the emotional edge. This time I let the tears flow and we hug each other tightly, neither of us wanting to let go.

'Come on, let's see if our room's ready' Andy says in a low voice, steering me gently towards the lift. Thank God we are the only people in there as we must look an odd pair - me with smudgy eye makeup and him, red eyed and blotchy faced.

Strangely enough, the sight of us in the lift mirror lightens the mood.

'Good lord, just look at the state of my eyes' I laugh, hunting in my hand bag for a tissue. Catching a glimpse of himself, Andy gives a big grin and before we know it we're both giggling hysterically. I guess it must be delayed shock or pent up nerves. Either way, I can't help noticing that he even laughs like Mr DJ, deep throated and lips curled in exactly the same way.

Once we are settled into the surprisingly colourful and informal meeting room, we can't stop talking. It's all a bit tentative at first, polite inquiries about each other's families, exchanges of photographs and a lot of talk about life in Toronto and Truro. We spend a long time talking about David, our long marriage and his early death.

'It must have been so hard to be widowed at such a young age.' Andy has gone into his doctor mode, sympathetic but treading carefully. I push the conversation back to Amy, my need to be strong for her, my admiration about how she has coped with David's death. Anything to change the subject.

I suspect he thinks I'm trying to avoid talking about my own grief. Little does he know that I'm actually suppressing my anger about David's affair.

'I must say you look even younger than in the photo you sent,' he says at one point staring straight across at me. It's disconcerting that he looks so like

Mr DJ.

'Well you're even more handsome in the flesh' I reply truthfully, stopping myself from adding 'just like your dad was.' He smiles, his face colouring slightly.

'Keep those compliments coming Debbie – just what the doctor ordered.' I love it that he has such an easy sense of humour, that's he's comfortable in his skin without being smug.   In this sense he reminds me of David, who had the same skill of putting everyone at their ease. Someone he would have got on so well with and will never now get to meet.

Over an hour passes before we move onto the bigger, more difficult discussion.

It's Andy who steers the conversation in this delicate direction.

'It must have been so difficult for you being pregnant at such a young age' he says, staring at the photograph I've brought along of me aged 15 with my friend Charlie.

Here we go - it has got to be faced.

'Yes, it was' I reply, also glancing down at my overly made up fifteen year old face. Little did I know when it was taken, that I'd be pregnant and living in the deepest South West of England before the year was out.

'And you felt that you couldn't tell your mum or

dad?' he asks, eyes still fixed on the younger me.

'No, sad as it sounds I couldn't. Things were so different back then. It was the 1970s but it might as well have been the 1950s where I lived. It was just easier to disappear, to hide away.' The tears are welling up again but I need to stay in control, to explain to Andy why I did what I did.

Andy looks up at me, his expression full of concern and pity.

'Yet you never once thought of abortion…?'

I pause for a moment, taken aback by the question.

'Sorry Debbie, I didn't mean to…' He reaches across and gives my hand another reassuring squeeze.

'No you are right to ask. And to answer your question, I never did consider a termination. Right from the start I decided that I had to go through with the pregnancy and then let someone else, in a much better position, take care of you.' It's no good trying to stem the tears now, and I reach across for a napkin to dab my eyes.

'Are you all right to carry on?' Andy asks, his voice cracking slightly.

'Yes, of course. It's important but you'll have to excuse me. You can imagine, after all these years of keeping things a secret….'

Andy pours me a glass of water as I brace myself for the question I know is coming next. He waits for me to compose myself before his words tumble out.

'And you never knew who my father was?'

I can't look him in the eye, so yet again I fix my gaze on the image of Charlie and me, posing in that photo booth all those years ago.

'No, I went to a party and was given a lot of alcohol. I wasn't used to it and got hopelessly drunk. One thing led to another, and all I remember is waking up the next day in a strange bedroom. I didn't even find out the young man's name…'

Surely Andy must know I'm lying, that there are tell tale signs?

'Well, I'm just so delighted to have met you Debbie and although it would be great to know about my dad, at least I've now found my birth mother.'

'Birth mother.' The words seem to echo around the room.

Before we know it, four hours have flown by and we are still here, emotionally drained but happy. Andy has been as delightful as I expected him to be, in fact even more so.

'Tell you what Debbie, I'm starved. Shall we head out to late lunch or just stay here?'

'Let's go out somewhere nice' I reply, adding that

lunch is on me.

He gives a mock grimace but can see that there is no point in arguing. As he heads off to his room to get his jacket, I've already come to my big decision.

I'm going to stay in touch with my son, come hell or high water.

No way am I going to lose him all over again.

Absolutely, no way.

Chapter 37

My Dilemmas…

You could say that life is all about dilemmas, constant decisions about which path to pursue when faced with a mind blowing array of routes. In Native American culture, there is something called 'Vision Quest', where time is taken out to ponder your next stage in life. It involves physical challenges like fasting and exploring difficult terrains, extended time alone to contemplate and when your path has been chosen, some sort of ceremony or ritual to confirm your decision. I read about it once and at the time thought it all sounded a bit hippy dippy, something I never was back in the 1970s. Actually, it makes some sort of sense now and if I had the option of jetting off to New Mexico for a few months of reflection and decision making, hell I might just be tempted.

As things stand, Cornwall will have to do and as my good mate Kevin has advised, it will have to be done one step at a time. I've always worked by the mantra, 'if in doubt, do nothing' but sometimes in life this just isn't an option. I'm also a great list maker and I find writing down things really does help, as it focuses the mind. So here I am, nearly 40 years since I last kept a diary, about to start a brand new one. Let's call it my 'dilemma diary', a sort of middle-aged confessional and it's even got a nifty lock on it, like my old teenage one. But this time it's made of smart pale blue suede and cost a small fortune from one of those posh stationery suppliers.

So my first entry is to write down those dilemmas. There are five big ones and if I'm really being truthful there's a sixth one as well.

Dilemma Number one – the road to take now I've finally met up with my son Andy. It's only a few days ago and we've already started making plans for me to visit him in Canada. To say I'm nervous about meeting his family is putting it mildly yet somehow I know in my heart that it will go well. Once I've returned from Canada, the next big question will have to be faced. Do I keep everything a secret between me, Andy and his adoptive parents? If I do this, will I just be repeating history, always living my life in the shadow of a lie?

Dilemma Number two – my daughter Amy. Without doubt she's my number one priority. If I tell her the truth about her brother, I risk losing her but if I don't say anything, I will go to my grave with a family secret that she could well discover afterwards. And how utterly devastating would that be?

Dilemma Number three – if I do tell Amy, then I

will need to involve my mum and sister who I've kept in the dark for decades. Mum isn't in great health and my fear is that the truth could kill her. As for my younger sister, who knows what it will do to our already fragile relationship.

Dilemma Number four – Mr DJ. He's Andy's dad and neither he nor my son even know it. I'm sure Andy is bound to keep thinking about this and in the meantime I'll need to persist with the fiction that I don't know who the father is. Whether I can keep this going in longer term, is another matter.

Dilemma Number five – the discovery of David's affair has shocked me to the core and has even left me questioning my own judgement and perception of the world. I'll never be able to sit him down and ask why. So should I pursue his mistress Jemma? Certainly, I can't foist this on Amy, who will have more than enough to cope with if I decide to tell her about Andy's existence. So given everything else going on in my life, is it best to take my best mate Kevin's advice and just let this one go? Can I be brave enough to do that?

Talking about Kevin, I've reached Dilemma Number Six. This one has just appeared over the past few days as we have bonded even more over our shared troubles. He's facing a messy divorce and is going for 50/50 custody of his two boys. Kevin has been a brilliant friend and confidante over the years and only once has our friendship spilled over into something more. At the time we both decided that our shared intimacy would be a one-off, something best buried and forgotten.

Whether it's to do with David's betrayal or something else, I don't really know. But suddenly the thought of being part of a couple again with Kevin, is starting to look more appealing. I miss the intimacy of a shared life, someone to come home to, cook meals with and cuddle up to late at night. Yes, you can have some of this with a good friend but it's not the same as living with someone under the same roof. So am I ready to take the plunge again if the chance arises?

I don't yet have answers to my dilemmas and I'm well aware that the paths I take will have a profound impact not just on my life but on all of the people involved, including my much loved daughter.

Now I need to start preparing for my trip to Canada to meet the people who took on my son all those decades ago, a child giving away her own child. One thing is certain – the choices I face will be even tougher than my teenage decision to hand over my baby.

So here's to the next stage of my life and what I'll call my 'Dilemma Quest'. Starting with a journey all the way from London to Toronto.

Maggie Fogarty

*To be continued - see what happens next
in the second book of the 'Dilemma Novella'
trilogy.*

Now that you have read this novella, would you
consider writing a review? Reviews are the best way
for readers to discover new books and will be
much appreciated.

And if you enjoyed this novella then do try the
novel 'My Bermuda Namesakes' or my short story
'Key' . See details and reviews on websites
www.maggiefogarty.com and
www.amazon.co.uk/www.amazon.com.

About the Author:

Maggie Fogarty is a Royal Television Society award winning television producer and journalist, making TV programmes for all the major UK broadcasters. She has also written extensively for a number of national newspapers and magazines.

In April 2011 her story 'Namesakes' was a finalist in the Writers and Artists/WAYB short story competition.

'My Bermuda Namesakes' was her debut novel and grew out of the original short story. It was written during a year long stay in Bermuda where Maggie's husband, Paul, was working as a digital forensics consultant. During her time on the island, Maggie wrote a guest column for the Bermuda Sun newspaper.

'Dear Mr DJ' is Maggie's second novel and forms part of a planned series called the 'Dilemma Novellas'.

The couple now live Cornwall in the far South West of England with their cockapoo dog Bonnie. Before moving there, they lived on the outskirts of Birmingham, in the English Midlands, where Maggie was born and grew up.

Author website: www.maggiefogarty.com

89655268R00122

Made in the USA
Columbia, SC
24 February 2018